CROWN OF YORK

CHARLOTTE BYRD

ABOUT CROWN OF YORK

He used to be my only hope. Easton Bay: **a man who's as ruthless as he's gorgeous and as tender as he is cruel.** His every touch sends shivers down my spine.

I crave him.

He saved me once, but will he do it again? He's a mystery. An enigma. A suspense.

There's a darkness inside of him. It scares me to my very core.

Yet, I pull closer with each breath. I am an addict and he is my drug.

What happens when it's not enough?

"Fast-paced, dark, addictive, and compelling" - Amazon Reviewer ★★★★★

"Hot, steamy, and a great storyline." - Christine Reese ★★★★★

"My oh my....Charlotte has made me a fan for life." - JJ, Amazon Reviewer ★★★★★

"The tension and chemistry is at five alarm level." - Sharon, Amazon reviewer ★★★★★

"Hot, sexy, intriguing journey of Elli and Mr. Aiden Black. - Robin Langelier ★★★★★

"Wow. Just wow. Charlotte Byrd leaves me speechless and humble... It definitely kept me on the edge of my seat. Once you pick it up, you won't put it down." - Amazon Review ★★★★★

"Sexy, steamy and captivating!" - Charmaine, Amazon Reviewer ★★★★★

" Intrigue, lust, and great characters...what more could you ask for?!" - Dragonfly Lady ★★★★★

HOUSE OF YORK SERIES READING ORDER

1. House of York
   2. Crown of York
   3. Throne of York
   4. Empire of York
   5. Demise of York

PART 1

CHAPTER 1 - EASTON

WHEN I TRY TO WASH IT ALL AWAY…

My life is a graveyard of things that I've done on my father's orders.

Now, deceiving Everly is just another tombstone.

I can't face her for what I've done. Mirabelle is here to take her to see my father. He will meet with all of the contestants, but he really wants to meet Everly.

He's aching to tell her. I know it.

I could be there to see the disappointment on her face. He had called me in as well, but this time, I won't come.

I can't bear to see her tear-misted eyes.

Why did I do it?

Why did I sleep with Everly? It would be a lie to

say that I only did it because of his orders. Deep down, I know that I had another motivation.

Everly.

When I first saw her at that charity ball, I was drawn to her immediately. There was something in her eyes. A glimmer. A twinkle.

And her demeanor? Uneasy and yet confident.

Then I spoke to her. Her voice was soft and distant, but familiar.

It was all of these things and so many more.

Everly smiled at me.

She challenged me.

She fought with me.

And suddenly, this connection we shared, became something *more*. We exchanged only a few pleasantries, but that was enough to strengthen our bond.

I TRIED TO PROTECT HER.

I tried to warn her about this place. I did the best I could without coming out and telling her everything. But she ended up here anyway; this dark, horrible piece of sand that is my home.

She shouldn't be here. None of them should. But she really shouldn't.

I was never much of a believer in destiny, and now I'm not so sure. Perhaps she is doomed to York just like I am.

Still, I cannot help myself. I know that there isn't much I can do for her, but I can't stop myself from trying.

She's pulling me toward her.

I crave her.

I want her.

I have to have her.

I haven't felt this way in years. Not since... It's still hard to talk about it.

There was once a woman in my life whom I loved very much. She knew what York was about. She and I tried to make a break from this place. We were going to spend the rest of our lives together, but then, she drowned.

I used to think that I had a curse on my head. I used to think that nothing good would ever happen to me or anyone else I know.

And now?

Now I know that I'm cursed for sure.

I descend under the water and push off the side

of the pool. I kick my legs as fast as I can to propel myself forward. I haven't swam in this pool in a long time, and I've forgotten how good it feels for water to run along your body.

Oh, if only I had the strength to submerge myself entirely and never come up for air again.

I tried to do that once. I should do it again before I cause any more suffering.

Unfortunately, I can't. I'm the only friend that Everly has and I can't leave her alone in this God-forsaken place.

As I split the turquoise water with my body, I imagine Everly walking toward my father on his throne. Even after all of these years, I cannot say that I know him well, but the one thing I do know is that he likes to play games.

My father takes a new wife every two years. He runs this competition to find her.

He is a rich, bored, old man who likes to pit people against each other in the illusion of a contest.

One will win, but what will she win exactly?

A lifetime of slavery?

Two years of being called a Queen, until the next one comes to replace her?

Everly is about to find out the truth about York.

5

She's about to find out that the only reason I slept with her is because he ordered me to. But I'm not sure if she will find out why I followed his orders.

I don't think he will tell her that it was in an effort to protect her. I don't think he will tell her that if I didn't, then she would be eliminated.

Everly March cannot be eliminated. Even if, at the end, she is to become my father's wife, I will do everything in my power to stop her from being eliminated and sold off at auction.

If she were to become Queen, she would live here in chains.

Not literal, but metaphorical.

She would be cloistered away with the rest of the wives.

She would have to travel with him.

She would have to attend formal functions.

She would have to sleep with him and bear his children.

She would not have much freedom, but she would not be sold off.

The rest of the contestants, the ones who will be eliminated until the Queen is crowned, will be auctioned off.

I don't know exactly what is to become of them, but I know that their lives will not be easy.

It will probably be akin to what's going on in the dungeons below. Foreign lands. Foreign rulers. Passed around as play things.

People around here talk in hushed tones about what awaits them.

I will do everything in my power to protect Everly from that life.

I flip over onto my back and tread water to stay afloat.

What did I ever do in my past life to deserve such a father? What did I ever do to deserve the life that I'm leading?

A part of me wishes I was more like Abbott. My brother is someone without much of a conscience. He lives entirely by his desires.

What he wants, he gets.

What he thinks he deserves, he goes after.

He doesn't care that none of the women here want him, or that they're all afraid of him. He likes the power that he has over them. He's the Prince of York, after all.

I'm a Prince of York as well, but what good does it do me? My heart goes out to the women who live behind York's gates, but I can't help them. I can't even show sympathy for them for fear that they will be punished as a result.

This place is a game that I can't win.

So, why do I keep trying?

What's the fucking point?

CHAPTER 2 - EASTON

WHEN I RUN INTO AN OLD FRIEND...

*E*verly does not return to me that day. A part of me wants to go find her. To tell her the truth, but another part knows that I can't.

I can't because he said I can't. He. The King of York. My fucking father.

Why did I ever come back here? Again, because of him. I don't come here often, but when I do, it's because I absolutely cannot miss the event. A lot of important people will be here. They will all be very impressed with my father and very happy to get some of his cast-offs. His hand-me-downs. The women he isn't interested in keeping for himself. Will Everly be one of them?

I know what I need to do. I need to stop thinking about her. There's a good chance she will be eliminated and I will never hear from her again. And, if she does become the Queen, well, then she will be my stepmother. Either way, it's dangerous to be her friend. But still, I can't keep her out of my mind.

After getting out of the water and toweling off, I decide to go for a run around the grounds. I don't go for any particular reason except that I need to do something with my body to get myself out of my head.

As blood starts to pump through my body faster and faster, I turn up the music on my phone and try to lose myself in my heavy breaths.

Breathe in.

Breathe out.

Breathe in.

Repeat.

Again.

Again.

Yet, my mind keeps going back to Everly.

Will my father really marry a woman who I just slept with?

Would he stoop that low?

And what about Abbott?

He was the one who attacked Everly, twice.

His first attack landed her in the dungeons. His

second attack landed him in Hamilton, a hard labor camp, for a week.

When he returns, he will be looking to exact his revenge. And he's not one who is easily satisfied.

As I make my way around the gardens with towering hedges and intricate flower arrangements, I turn down a small alleyway toward the back of the main mansion. This is my quiet place, somewhere I can be alone with my thoughts. I slow down to a jog and enjoy the sight of a few hummingbirds gathering around a little bush. A little bit to the side of them, a finch pounces around, looking for crumbs, near the rose bushes.

Just then, a large double door swings open and a woman with hair in a shawl comes out.

Stunned to see her, I trip over my feet and collide straight into her before either of us can move out of the way.

"Oh, I'm sorry," I mumble, a little dazed.

I look around and see that I have knocked her all the way to the ground. "Are you okay?"

"Yes, yes, I'm fine," she whispers, averting her eyes.

I give her my hand to help her up, but she rejects it. Instead, she gets up on her own. Wait a second. I know who she is. At least, I think I do.

"Isla?" I ask, kneeling down to get a better look at her face.

She looks up at me. Our eyes meet for a second, but then she looks down at the ground again. Yes, it is her.

"Isla, it's me, Easton."

"Yes, of course, your Royal Highness," she mumbles. She bows her head before me and bends at the knee. A perfectly-executed curtsy.

"Do you remember me?" I press her.

"I'm sorry, your highness, but I have to go," she says and takes a few steps back. Technically, she is not allowed to turn her back on my face, so if she wants to walk away, she has to retreat away from me.

I take a few steps forward. I'm not going to let her get away that easily.

"Isla—" I start to say.

"Please, don't call me that, your highness," she whispers under her breath. I can see the terror in her eyes. What has he done to her to make her so afraid?

"I haven't seen you in a long time," I say. "How are you?"

"I'm wonderful," she lies.

As she turns a little away from me, her loose-fitting floor-length day dress with long sleeves snags on her stomach. I see that it's bulging out past the rest of her rather small body.

I look at her and wonder what became of the spunky, fun girl who came to babysit me when I was little.

She was the daughter of one of my father's closest friends. But after his sudden death, she was one of the first participants in the original contest that my father held to find his first Queen. She won and her prize was to marry him and have his children.

"Are you pregnant?" I ask.

"Yes, your highness."

"Again?"

"Yes, your highness," she says, looking sullen and tired.

"How far along are you?"

"Seven months, your highness."

"But didn't you just have one?"

"I had two ten months ago, your highness."

"So, how many is that now?"

She looks up at me and forces herself to smile. "I am the proud mother of seven children, your highness. With one on the way, your highness."

I can see that she has been lying for so long that

she no longer knows what is true or what is a lie. Or maybe at this point, she barely cares.

"And my father doesn't think he's had enough?"

"Your father is a lover of children, your highness," she says proudly.

Yeah, right, I say to myself. He has so many children that I've lost count and I'm pretty sure that he has, too. It's as if he thinks that the survival of the planet depends on him.

"Thank you for stopping to talk to me, your highness," Isla says and takes a few steps away from me.

I want to talk to her, and I can demand that she does. But what would be the point?

I watch her retreat, and I don't follow her.

CHAPTER 3 - EASTON

WHEN I HAVE TO SEE HER...

*I*sla's name isn't Isla anymore. It is not enough for my father to take away a person's rights and to make her a captive for life. He also has to erase her whole identity.

He changed her name to Eleanor on their wedding day. It is forbidden for me and everyone else to use the name Isla, but she will always be Isla to me.

Spunky and feisty and a little dangerous, Isla once showed me how to practice kissing someone on my arm. She looks up at me one last time before she disappears around the corner.

I realize that I don't know that woman anymore. As a stepmother with seven children and one on the way, she is a stranger. It's not because she's a mother or the fact that she has so many kids. She's a stranger because living at York for so many years, she has become a shell of the person she was once.

I see her body.

I see her face.

But I no longer see her spirit. She used to have this enthusiasm for life, an excitement that she could never contain.

But it's gone now.

Probably for good.

I have not seen Isla in a long time and I wonder how long it will be before I see her again. She is no longer *the* Queen, just *a* Queen. The title of *the* Queen belongs to my father's most recent wife. But she retains her seniority.

Just like with everything else here, my father's wives have rules which guide their behavior. Prior to marriage, they all wore short dresses, strapless bikinis, and high heels, but not now.

Now, they are his property and no one is to see them as he sees them.

They are no longer allowed to show any skin and have to wear clothes that cover them up from head to toe. They even have to wear a shawl over their hair.

They are also mainly sequestered to another part

of his house. While Abbott and I have free reign of the place, my father's wives barely exist. Everything is brought to them in their chambers and they rarely venture outside.

I wish there was something I could do to help them, but what? This place is bigger than all of us. The darkness that resides here will be the end of all of us one day.

* * *

DESPITE MY BETTER JUDGEMENT, I can't help but head back to the main house. I want to get a glimpse of Everly, if only for a moment. I can't explain anything about what I did or why I did it. I seduced her on someone's orders. I did it to save her life. Or at least, prolong it temporarily.

There are certain things in life, you just have to do.

Even if they are futile.

And stupid.

And unlikely to result in a desirable outcome.

There are things you just have to do, just because.

When I get to the front door, I don't bother knocking. Instead, I open the door and head upstairs. I know which room is hers. When I get to her door, I pause. A pang of fear rushes through me. What will I see on the other side?

I knock lightly.

"Who is it?"

"Easton."

She doesn't say anything for a moment and then the door opens.

Everly is dressed in a long sleeping gown and a thin silk robe. Her eyes meet mine.

"Come in," she says coldly.

"Everly...I wanted to talk to you," I say. I need to apologize, but the words don't come.

"How can I help you?" she asks, sitting on the edge of the bed.

There's a darkness emanating from her, the kind that follows disappointment.

"You have to understand," I start to say.

"Yes?"

"You have to understand that I wanted to spend the night with you."

She nods.

"Do you understand?"

"Yes, I do," she says, clenching her jaw.

She doesn't.

Of course, she doesn't.

But what can I say?

How can I explain this without actually explaining this?

"Your father was kind enough to inform me about everything that is going on here," she says after a moment.

"He did?"

"He said that you were ordered to do what you did."

I nod.

"Well, he's the King. So, I understand."

"So...what about now?"

"Easton, I don't know what you want from me," she says after a moment. "I'm here to participate in a contest. A contest, I have the feeling that I have to win. Whatever happened between us was just part of the game, right?"

"Right," I mumble. What else is there to say?

"Well, good. Thank you for coming. I'm sure that I will see you around."

She ushers me toward the door.

"And you're not...mad?"

"Mad? No, of course not," she says, closing the door in my face.

So, why don't I believe you? I ask under my breath and walk away.

Frankly, I don't know why I even bothered. How did I expect this meeting to go?

At the bottom of the stairs, I see Mirabelle, my father's trusted advisor and assistant. She has been with him for years.

"Oh, hello sir, it's very nice to see you," she says loudly.

I nod and try to make my way past her. But suddenly, her arm brushes against mine and I hear her clear her throat.

"You need to stay away from her," she whispers under her breath while covering her lips with her hand. "If you want to protect her, stay away from her."

CHAPTER 4 - EVERLY

WHEN THERE'S A KNOCK ON MY DOOR...

The thing about captivity is that there's this tendency to reach out and try to hang onto anyone who shows you a meager amount of kindness.

Your decisions aren't your own.

Your life belongs to someone else.

You are powerless.

And then, when someone comes along and shows you that maybe you do have a friend, maybe you can trust someone, you tend to believe them.

You tend to go out of your way to trust them.

But why?

I sit in my room at the desk and put these words onto paper.

There's something about writing that crystalizes

my thoughts. It puts all the chaos that is swirling in my head into organized concrete ideas. It's funny to say this, but I often don't even know that I'm thinking about something until I begin to write. Then as the words start to flow out of me, they form an opinion and suddenly I come to an understanding of what it is I'm thinking.

So, why is it that I was so eager to give my heart to Easton?

He had helped me a few times, but he had also betrayed me. The truth is that I don't really know anything about him.

He told me some story about a woman he loved and showed his vulnerabilities.

But what did that mean anyway?

Maybe that was a lie, just like everything else here? Everything about York is just one big deceit.

I have to be stronger from now on. I have to play the game, just like they are playing a game, that is if I want to win. And to play the game right, I have to have the element of surprise on my side.

There's a knock on my door.

When I open it, I see him.

Easton.

His head is hanging low. His eyes are refusing to meet mine. He knows that I know.

He is here to apologize, make amends.

Or maybe this is just another move in the game?

I take a deep breath and put on a metaphorical mask. I will not let him see my true feelings. I will keep him out.

We exchange words for a few minutes. I keep my head high and my chin pointed toward the ceiling. Nothing he says will make the proud expression on my face wane or change in any way.

"And you're not...mad?" Easton asks. I stare at him.

Mad is beyond what I am right now.

My whole body is tingling from rage. It's building deep inside my core and spreading to the extremities. But again, I don't show one bit of this. Not a single molecule of my rage escapes from within me.

"Mad? No, of course not," I say and shut the door in his face.

As soon as I'm alone in the room, tears start to stream down my face. Each one is hot, fueled by the fire coming from the pit of my stomach.

How could he ask me that?

How could he toy with me like that?

Why didn't he apologize?

Why did he even come here if he wasn't going to say he's sorry?

No, no, no.

Get a hold of yourself, Everly.

You are better than this.

Stronger than this.

Easton is an illusion.

You don't know the first thing about him. Or this place. It is very possible that he is more cruel and cunning than Abbott.

What if he is only playing the part of a nice guy?

What if that's part of his act?

No, from now on, I will trust no one but myself. I will rely on no one but myself.

I will assume that everyone here has an agenda, including me.

What's my agenda?

To survive.

By any means possible.

I PUT DOWN THE PEN. Yes, that's right. Of course, that's right. I have to survive.

I mean, what's the alternative? Death?

That option will be there no matter what.

And I'm sure that it will come soon enough.

But for now, I have to fight.

The thing about life is that it's all about perspective, isn't it? I have seen the worst of York down in the dungeons. Now, imprisonment up here doesn't seem that bad.

My body may still not be entirely my own, but there are no chains, or groups of men, or the screams.

Everything here is civilized.

A civilized kind of captivity, if you will.

Given what I've been through, I can make it here.

I don't know if I can make it all the way, but I have to give it my best shot.

I look at four pieces of paper which I filled up with my lackluster handwriting - ugly small loops, lazy half-finished words - basically, scribbles. I've always wanted to have that beautiful handwriting you see in nineteenth century letters. Each loop of the pen painstakingly loved and adored.

But for that, I would need to have time and patience. And when the words are gushing out of me, I have neither.

Suddenly, something occurs to me.

These pieces of paper are the only things that I own in this whole place.

I don't own any of the clothes or the shoes or the makeup.

Frankly, I don't even own my body. But these pieces of paper are mine.

The words that I have written on them have transformed this generic notepad with the House of York stamp at the top into something precious; my story.

I press the paper to my chest and cherish the moment.

It's too bad I can't hold onto them.

No one can see what I have written and there's only one way to keep my thoughts safe. Ripping the pages up and tossing them away in the trash is not enough.

I fold each piece in half and then in half again. I then rip it along the creases.

The paper is thin and it rips fast.

I put pieces of it in my mouth and swallow, chasing them down with gulps of water.

Now, my thoughts are safe.

PART 2

CHAPTER 5 - EVERLY

WHEN I'M SURPRISED...

We have dinner downstairs, family style. A chef is brought in to cook the food and waiters are there to serve it. We sit at one long table with a white tablecloth draped over it. Elegant and expertly designed centerpieces grace the middle, equal distances from each other.

I don't know much about flowers, but they look like lilies to me. Each stalk is wrapped in baby's breath. Waiters are making their way around with bottles of wine and champagne. I find my name plate, or rather, number plate, and sit down. My friend Paige waves at me from across the table and I nod back.

I'm glad she isn't sitting right next to me. I find it difficult to meet new people when I already have someone to talk to. And I need to make an effort to get to know the others.

"Hi, I'm Olivia," the girl next to me whispers.

"I'm Everly," I whisper back. "Aren't we supposed to go by numbers?"

She shrugs. "I don't really like that much."

"Me neither."

While we dig into our salads, I find out that Olivia is a fellow Pennsylvanian. She grew up in Pittsburgh, in a wealthy enclave called Fox Chapel, where the Heinz family still has a home. She graduated from the best private school in the area and even boarded there the last two years of high school when her parents took off on an extended world cruise.

"Did you mind doing that?" I ask her.

"No, not at all. It was actually kind of cool. The boarders had the run of the place after school and it felt a lot like living in a dorm."

After graduating, Olivia went to Brown in Rhode Island and majored in English. She did her senior thesis on Elizabethan playwrights - "Not Shakespeare!" - as she pointed out.

"You really don't need to clarify," I say with a smile on my face. "I actually took a free online course called Not Shakespeare from Oxford last summer."

"Really?" She sits up in her seat. I nod.

"You know, not that many people know about anyone else from that time."

"Most people barely know about Shakespeare," I laugh.

For some reason, I'm unable to contain my arrogance in the presence of someone who shares my obscure interest.

"Spenser's *Faerie Queen* is one of my favorites," I add.

"I'm partial to Christopher Marlow's work," she adds and we both crack up laughing.

I want to ask Olivia about how she ended up here, but I sense that the timing for this question isn't quite right. I wouldn't be able to tell her the truth about my story anyway.

When Olivia gets up to use the restroom, I turn to the girl on the other side of me.

Unlike Olivia, with her thick chocolate hair, Savannah has a much spunkier shoulder-length hairstyle. Her hair is the color of caramel and a perfect complement to her blue-green eyes.

Savannah is taller than Olivia and me, with wide,

toned shoulders and a long neck. She has full lips, which glisten in the light.

"Where are you from?" I ask after I go over some sketches from my bio.

"Boston. Well, Nantucket, but really Boston."

I laugh.

"We spend summer on Nantucket, so all of my best memories are from there. Doesn't that count as a place where you're from?"

I shrug. "I don't really know. We spend a week on the Gulf Coast each summer, but I wouldn't say I'm from Florida."

Her face tenses up and forms a little crease in between her eyebrows.

"Oh, I'm sorry, I really didn't mean to offend you. I was just joking," I say quickly. "I think I've had a few too many of these."

I raise my glass of white wine.

"No worries. at all." Savannah waves her hand at me. "Well, just for the record, my family has a house in Nantucket and we spend three months there every summer. Most of my friends are from there."

"Then it counts!"

As we talk, I learn that Savannah's father lost most of the family's money a few years ago after a start-up that he had invested in heavily went under, and they had to declare bankruptcy. The house in Nantucket is no more. Along with the main house in Boston. Her parents divorced soon after, and her mom moved down to Miami to live with her own mother. She doesn't know where her father is, but she suspects that he had to disappear if he wanted to keep a cent of his money.

"So, you haven't heard from him?" I ask. She shakes her head proudly.

"Not once."

"And you think he's still...okay?" I ask.

I don't want to use the word, dead, because it seems too morbid. Though this is, of course, a real possibility.

"Occasionally, I get strange things in the mail. Little gifts from various places around the world. Like trinkets. A bracelet from Malta. A gold ring from Bhutan. Things like that. No return address. No message inside."

"So, that's how you know it's from him?"

She nods.

I want to ask her more, but it doesn't feel right. She doesn't want to talk about it so I drop it. When Olivia returns to the table, dessert is served. Tall, intricate chocolate cakes with little chocolate swirls on top. Each one is carried by individual servers and carefully placed in front of us.

Thanking my server for mine, I glance at the one next to him. Our eyes meet and he quickly darts away.

Wait a second.

He looks just like him.

No, that can't be him.

The man places the plate in front of Savannah and walks away without acknowledging me.

"Jamie?" I whisper.

CHAPTER 6 - EVERLY

WHEN I CAN'T BELIEVE MY EYES...

The server leaves so quickly I barely have a chance for another look, but I'm certain that it's him. Jamie.

What's his last name again?

I search my mind, but nothing comes up. I can't remember.

What I do remember is every outline of his face and the melodic texture of his voice.

What I do remember is how sorry I felt that he was worrying about me after I had disappeared.

What I do remember is he's a liar and an asshole who is responsible for me ending up here.

But why?

Why did he do it?

And what is he doing here now, working as a server?

Who are you, Jamie?

I know enough about this place to know that that's probably not his real name.

"I'll be right back." I gracefully excuse myself and make my way around the table.

"You better come back quickly!" Paige yells after me. "Otherwise, I'm pretty sure that I'll finish off your dessert along with mine."

Glancing back at her, I laugh. She's not kidding. Her falling tower of chocolate is nearly gone and she has her eye on mine.

The long black gown that I'm dressed in is uncomfortable. It's binding my legs together and it's so tight around my waist that it's creating the illusion of a perfect hour-glass figure.

Before I got to York, I'd never had the opportunity to wear anything like this. You know what I mean; anything really nice.

I've been to Saks Fifth Avenue a few times, just out of curiosity, but I've never tried anything on.

What would be the point? I couldn't afford any of those dresses anyway and I didn't want to waste the sales assistant's time.

Looking back, the reason I never enjoyed shopping for clothes much is that I've always been uncomfortable in my skin. The clothes I did try on at discount stores never fit quite right and I always assumed that it was because my body was so... misshapen.

But the thing is that I now realize that it wasn't my body at all.

It was the wrapping I was trying to adorn it with.

When Mirabelle came with the stylist and the array of outfits for me to try on, I suddenly realized that it was the duty of the clothes to fit me, not for me to fit the clothes.

Of course, I still wish some parts of me were smaller or tighter or had less cellulite, but all in all, higher-end clothes had a much better fit. And if they didn't have a good fit right from the beginning, the seamstress fixed it right away.

Do you want it tighter here?

Looser there? My wish was her command.

And the final result?

I glance at myself in the hallway mirror.

The black dress with delicate beading complements my body in every possible way. It shapes it into having a small waist and plumper butt. The heart-shaped neckline brings my breasts up to the heavens without cutting off my breathing or making any other part of me, especially in the back, bulge out.

I have no idea how much this dress costs out there in the real world, but right now it makes me feel like a million bucks. And I appreciate that.

The mirrored hallway is distracting since it serves as a reminder that I've never looked this good before.

But I try to focus my attention on the task at hand; Jamie.

Where did he go?

How can I find him?

After making sure that he is not hiding in this area of the house, I head back toward the main dining hall. I check the kitchen again, and then the area just outside where other servers are gathering. He's nowhere to be found.

Suddenly, I see someone sneaking into the bathroom across the hallway, near the rear entrance. From the back, it could very well be him, but I have to get closer to make sure.

I knock on the door and the man's voice says, "Occupied."

Just with that one word, I know that it's him.

I haven't heard it in I don't know how long and yet it's timbre and tone is etched into my mind.

CHARLOTTE BYRD

It belongs to a man I thought would change my life. He did, just not in the way I imagined.

I wait patiently outside without another word until he comes out. He emerges, wiping his hands on the back of his pants.

"Hello, Jamie," I say, stopping him dead in his tracks.

I wait for him to say something, but he doesn't. Does he think he can make me disappear by ignoring me?

"Well, I'm here," I say, crossing my arms across my chest. He runs his fingers across his hair and looks down at the floor.

"How's your grandmother doing?" I ask.

Again, he says nothing.

At first, I liked the power that I had over him. I liked that I could make him squirm. But then it starts to get irritating.

I have questions.

I deserve answers.

"Aren't you going to say anything?" I demand to know.

"I need to get back to work," Jamie says, walking around me and heading straight into the kitchen.

"Are you just going to pretend I'm not here?" I yell after him.

38

"I don't know what you're talking about," he mumbles.

I follow him closely, unsure as to what to do next.

I want to punch him.

I want to pull his hair and kick him as hard as I can. But something is holding me back.

CHAPTER 7 - EVERLY

WHEN THERE'S ANOTHER TEST...

*A*s Jamie disappears into the kitchen, I try one last time.

"It's you, Jamie, I know it's you!" I yell after him.

I resist every urge in my body and do not attack him.

I have to play this smart.

They know that he was the one who got me here.

Is that why he's the one serving us dinner? Is this a test? Are they doing this to find out how I'd react?

Instead of following him, I go back to my seat and see that Paige has already started in on my dessert, despite Olivia's best efforts.

"It's okay," I joke. "You can have all of it."

"No, she cannot," Savannah pipes in. "This is the

most delicious thing I've ever tasted and it would be a travesty if you didn't have a bite."

I nod and plunge my fork into the toppled-over tower of chocolate. Despite the fact that my mouth is quickly conquered by a confectionary masterpiece, I try to focus on the task at hand.

"Wow, this is delicious," I mumble and nod through the bites.

"Told you." Savannah laughs. "Now, you owe me."

The girls start to chat about the dinner and the contest to come. Everyone seems genuinely excited to find out about the next stage in the process, probably not knowing that we are already smack in the middle of one.

I'm sure that *they* are watching. Passing judgement. But what is there to gauge from a dinner?

Our table manners? How well we interact with others?

A few moments later, the servers emerge. Dressed in black and white tuxedos and with tails, they resemble a line of penguins. Their hair and facial expressions are identical. None of them are meant to stand out from the pack.

Yet, I spot Jamie immediately.

Third from the back.

He is cowering a bit, not walking with his head held high like the rest.

Is he expecting a reaction from me? An attack? An assault?

"Jamie?!" A shriek emanates from somewhere near me.

It's so high and shrill that it takes me a moment to realize that it's coming from Paige. Another moment later, she's on her feet and waving her arms.

"What the hell are you doing here?" she yells, throwing herself at him.

When they collide, the bottle that Jamie is holding falls to the floor and shatters. Red liquid mixes with glass and spreads along the tiles, quickly filling in the grout.

When I reach her, Paige is slapping Jamie across the face over and over. He is pushing her away from him without much success.

"Paige, stop, stop, please," I whisper in her ear and grab one of her arms. She manages to break free and clock him right in the face. When her fist collides with his chin, his legs let go from under him. No longer in any control, his feet swing up into the air and he lands on his back onto the glass.

"Aghh!" he yells out in pain.

"Serves you right, you asshole!" Paige yells and kicks him in his ribs. "What the fuck are you doing here?"

Tears stream down her cheeks and mix with the mascara and foundation running down her face.

Her anguish produces thick, all consuming sobs which echo around the dining room.

Silence falls as everyone listens and waits, unsure as to what to do next.

Despite how much pleasure it gives me to watch her heels kick Jamie in the ribs, I pull Paige away from him.

"I'm sorry, I'm so sorry," I apologize to the other girls and the waiters.

I don't need to, of course. I've done nothing wrong, but the apology is really for those people whom I can't see.

I can feel them judging Paige and I don't want them to judge her too harshly.

"You don't know who this is, Everly," Paige whispers. "He's..."

"Shh," I say, putting my hand over her lips.

"He's—"

"Shhh," I whisper. "Please don't say anything else. Please."

As I plead, Paige's eyebrows furrow and she looks at me with devilish eyes.

"Wait a second! What's going on here?" she demands. "Why are you trying to calm me down? Why aren't you on my side?"

I don't have an answer. When she told me about Jamie before and that he was her way in, I didn't tell her my own story. I didn't know if she had experienced the horrors of this place and I'd made that mistake already with Alessandra, so I didn't want to make the same one with Paige.

"Why are you protecting him?" Paige asks, pushing my hands away from her.

"Paige, please, calm down," I say. "Let's just try to clean this place up and continue with dinner."

"How could you be such a fake? I thought you were my friend!"

"I am."

"So... why? Why aren't you asking me why I did that?" Her shock is making her stutter and trip over her words. There are so many things I want to say to her, but I can't. Not if I want both of us to make it past this round.

"He's the guy you met earlier, right?" I ask, carefully picking my words. "The one who didn't call you for a while?"

I'm grasping at straws. I can't remember if this was actually what she told me, but I need to give her a good excuse for attacking him. Maybe she was just a jilted ex? Not really a girlfriend but someone who expected a call or a text if they were going to stop seeing each other.

This seems to calm her down and the anger I see in her eyes starts to subside.

CHAPTER 8 - EVERLY

WHEN THERE'S ANOTHER TEST…

I kneel down to help clean up some of the mess. In the fight, two other servers went down along with the bottles that they were holding. Red wine mixed with white wine and broken glass makes for a mosaic of destruction.

As I pick up pieces of the broken glass, the servers soak up wine with paper towels. Jamie stands up and glares at Paige. She stands on the other side of me, cradling her hand.

"Are you okay?" I ask.

"My hand hurts," she says.

"You hit him pretty hard," I whisper and can't help but snicker. She shouldn't have punched him, but I'm glad he got punched.

He deserved it.

He deserves a lot more than that.

"You really don't have to clean," one of the servers says when I hand him two handfuls of glass.

"It's okay, really."

"I wouldn't want you to get hurt," he adds.

I glance up at him.

Is this a joke?

Is he mocking me?

Cutting my hands on some glass is the least of my worries. I scrutinize his face for a tinge of mockery, but I don't find any.

You're just being paranoid, Everly. Stop it. This guy didn't mean anything.

I know that I don't need to clean, but I have to do something. I need to keep my hands busy so that I can have a few minutes to think about what to say next. And that's exactly why I wish that Paige would help me.

"Here, Paige, why don't you soak up some of this wine," I say, handing her the roll of paper towels.

"No," she says, shaking her head.

Another server runs over, grabs it, and quickly does the job for her. I look up at her. It's as if she's in a trance, staring at the wine spread from one paper towel square to the next. I touch her to snap her out of it.

"What the hell, Everly?" Paige jumps away from me.

I get up and walk over to her. I get really close so that hopefully only she can hear me.

"What are you doing?" I whisper.

"You have no idea what you're talking about, Everly. You don't know who that guy is!"

I clench my jaw and collect my thoughts.

"He's the guy who never wanted to sleep over at your place? The one who is living with his grandmother, right?"

She looks at me with surprise.

"He's the one who took you to that exclusive party at the Elliott Hotel in New Haven?"

She nods again. I think I have said enough.

"The thing is that I didn't tell you the whole story," she whispers.

"Don't start now," I say, barely under my breath. She looks surprised.

Glancing back, I see them sitting at the table, pretending to mind their own business. Some are picking at their desserts, others are sipping their drinks.

It's all a facade, a game of pretend.

In reality, everyone in this room, all the contestants and the servers, are listening and waiting.

I can't tell her not to say another incriminating word.

"The thing is that you are just mad at the fact that he never called you again," I say in the most lighthearted way possible.

"Right?" I nudge her.

She shrugs.

"Right, Paige?" I ask, taking her by the elbow and actually shaking her a little bit.

She continues to glare in Jamie's direction.

"Don't look at me like that!" he yells. "I was just doing my job!"

This breaks whatever tension I was managing to keep at bay and sends Paige into overdrive.

"Your job! You were just doing your job! What the hell are you talking about?" she roars across the room.

"I was supposed to bring you there, okay? They told me to."

"So, what are you doing here?" she asks. "Working as a server?"

49

"This is my job, too. I'm a paid intern. I do what they tell me to do."

His job?

A paid internship?

He was actually hired to trick me into going to that event? But why?

I look at the women around me and I see them thinking as well. How many of them did he lure here as well? I wonder.

When I see two men in dark suits and radios in their ears appear in the hallway, I know that Jamie said too much. They block the entire entrance with their massive bodies and slowly make their way toward us.

"I'm sorry. I didn't mean to say that," Jamie says when they crowd around him.

Paige takes a step back.

And then another step.

And another.

When I turn back toward Jamie, I see one of the security guards pulling him out of the room.

"I'll get her!" the other one yells and takes off after Paige, who already disappeared.

I follow Olivia out of the dining room into the foyer.

"No, let me go," Paige mumbles into the floor

with the guard sitting on her back, holding her arms behind her back. He reaches into his back pocket and places a pair of handcuffs on her.

"If you're not going to come nicely, I'm not going to do this nicely," he hisses.

I shake my head in disbelief.

"Where is he taking her? Why?" I ask.

Olivia looks as dumbfounded as I feel.

"They're not going to hurt her, are they?" Savannah asks.

We exchange looks.

I peer into her eyes to get a glimpse of what she actually knows. But I don't see anything except terror.

"Let me go!" Paige yells at the top of her lungs as she struggles to get away. The guard holds her tightly to his body and pushes her down the stairs with his knee.

"Everly! I'm sorry, Everly!"

It takes everything within me to not run after her or try to pry that guard from her.

"I'm sorry, too," I say. Tears start to stream down her face.

"It's going to be okay, Paige," I say. She shakes her head.

"This place..." she mumbles through her sobs.

"This place isn't what you think it is, Everly. You have to get out of here!"

The guard walks her out of the room and one of the servers shuts the doors behind them.

WHEN WE WAIT...

My mind runs in circles as we stand around the room waiting. Someone tries the double doors, but they are locked.

Dinner is officially over.

The other contestants talk among themselves, rehashing the events of the day, but I can't bear to utter a word.

What just happened?

It seemed to have happened in slow motion, yet in an instant.

One moment, I was running after Jamie and the next, Paige is punching him and knocking him to the floor.

But what about after that? The guards. One

pulling him away, the other putting handcuffs on her.

She knew.

She knew more about this place all along.

Why didn't she tell me? For the same reason I didn't tell her.

I couldn't.

I couldn't risk it.

I couldn't risk being eliminated or being thrown into the dungeon again.

Could she?

Was that why she attacked him?

Did she go through what I went through?

My thoughts continue to run on overdrive in my head. Questions appear and collide with one another. There's no time to think up suitable answers.

"I can't believe they arrested her," Savannah whispers in my ear. I nod, still unable to speak.

"I mean, I know that she hit him hard, but did they really need to take her down like that?"

I shrug.

"It's almost as if she were a terrorist."

"Well, a terrorist would probably get shot," Olivia adds.

No, a terrorist sits on the throne of York, I want to

say, but I bite my tongue.

"What do you think is going to happen to her?"
I ask.

Olivia and Savannah exchange looks. I don't
know them well enough to read them.

Do they know something I don't?

Or is it just a regular look of shock on their faces?

I want to ask them directly.

What was it like for them?

Had they also met Jamie before they ended
up here?

But I know that I can't.

"What do you think Paige meant by what she
said?" I ask. I know that they heard her. They
all did.

"That this place isn't what we think it is?" Olivia
asks.

I watch her carefully, trying my best to read into
every one of her facial expressions.

If l learned one thing from my degree in
psychology, it is that people say so much more by
their body language than they do by their words.
And the best psychologists are the ones who can
read into this language. Too bad I'm not one. I can't
glean a thing from Olivia.

"She was probably just making empty threats,"

Savannah says. "I mean, she kind of lost it when she saw him, didn't she? Who is he?"

Now, I turn to Savannah, but her face offers even less clues than Olivia's.

The skin is perfectly smooth around her eyes, without a single crinkle of confusion or disillusionment.

As we talk, I can't help but wonder if they know the truth about this place just like I do. Or at least, a glimpse of the truth.

I mean, prior to Paige's outburst, I never once considered the possibility that she knew more about York than she let on. She was such a good actress.

Are Olivia and Savannah thinking the same thing about me right now?

Are they wondering how it is that I'm maintaining my composure and acting like everything is fine knowing what I know?

A few minutes later, one of the large double doors swings open and J, the host of the event, enters.

He looks just as dashing and confident as ever, if not a bit tired.

When he smiles at us, little dimples form on the sides of his cheeks.

He calls out to get our attention even though he

doesn't need to. We all immediately stand in a semi-circle in front of him and wait.

"I'm sorry that you all had to witness that," he says after clearing his throat.

Unlike before when he was completely confident and effortless in his delivery, now something is flustering him. It's almost as if he is a bit lost.

Or maybe even unsure.

He refers to Paige by her number and then by her name, seesawing back and forth, as if he had forgotten his place.

"As you all saw, Paige attacked one of the servers for virtually no reason," he says, going with her name this time.

Bullshit, I say to myself.

"The organization here was not aware of the fact that they had previous contact and that they in fact saw each other socially."

Double bullshit.

You weren't aware of their previous contact?

Or the fact that they saw each other socially?

You mean, he supposedly dated her and me and took us to the Bay Foundation charity ball all on his own?

"Again, I apologize for the fact that you had to see her put into handcuffs like that and escorted out.

We do not condone anyone putting their hands on each other here and as a result she had to leave," J says.

So, it's okay for other people in the organization to put their hands on us, but not for us to fight back? I want to say.

"But she wasn't really arrested, was she?" someone from the back asks.

J takes a deep breath, probably trying to decide the best way to formulate his answer.

"Well, no, of course not," he says after a moment. "Unless the server decides to press charges. For now, she was just eliminated from the competition."

Eliminated.

There's that word again.

In this place, it's synonymous with a fate worse than death.

WHEN WE HAVE ANOTHER SURPRISE...

J don't know what awaits Paige, but I am afraid to even think about it. It is my worst nightmare, except for my own elimination.

While I'm here, I have a chance.

A chance at what I'm not exactly sure, but perhaps a life that doesn't so much resemble hell.

And as for Paige? I don't know.

I don't know what waits her *there*. But if it's something that even Mirabelle talks about in a hushed tone, then I know it comes with a lot of fear.

J continues to drone on about what just supposedly happened to Paige to make her act out. The contempt that I used to feel for him decreases.

He's just another pawn in this game. He's only

looking out for himself and I can't really blame him. That's exactly what I'm doing.

That's the only thing really, to do in this place.

"Okay, well, that's enough about all that unpleasantness," J says. "I am actually here with a little bit of a surprise for you, ladies."

Everyone's eyes light up with excitement. When Olivia turns to me, I pretend that I can't wait to see what it is either.

"Okay, why don't you line up here, one next to another." J spreads his hands and we divide ourselves into two even groups.

Five on each side.

Is that all the girls who are left?

I've never counted everyone before, but now... now, the numbers are dwindling down, there are few enough to count.

Once everyone is in position, J turns himself to the front door. Mirabelle and all the servers, except for one, gather behind him.

A moment later, the door swings open and the King enters.

He looks exactly like the man I saw sitting upon that silver velvet high-back throne.

He is dressed in a similarly expensive and

exquisitely tailored three-piece suit, which accentuates his fit, slender physique.

He narrows his eyes as he presents himself to us and Mirabelle curtsies before him.

I quickly follow her lead and so do the rest of the contestants.

"That was quite an event, wasn't it, girls?" he asks in a condescending manner.

He does not use the word girls to be playful or fun, but rather to demean us. But if that's the most belittling thing he does, that would be a joy.

I somehow doubt it.

He adjusts his stand and crosses his hands in front of him. His cufflinks sparkle in the evening light. The chandelier above our heads illuminates the whole room completely, while maintaining the intensity of light candlelight. Even the lights here are rich.

"I just wanted to introduce myself and welcome you to York. Personally," he continues when we all rise to our feet. "Yes, I am the King of York, but I also have a name. Alistair Bay."

The name Alistair explains the light English accent. It's not exactly a name that's popular in America.

Alistair Bay.

As in the Bay Foundation.

Of course.

He walks over to the girl at the far end of the line and picks up her hand. Mirabelle motions to her to curtsy and she does what she is told, even though the execution comes out rather clumsy.

The King lifts up her hand to his lips and kisses the back of it.

"It's a pleasure to meet you," he says.

"The pleasure is all mine," she giggles in return.

He makes his way down the line and then finally gets to me.

"Ah, we meet again, Everly March," he says, taking my hand to his lips.

a , but he mentions my name.

I must've made an impression, but I'm not sure if that's a good or a bad thing.

"It's very nice to see you again," I lie and bend my knees slightly before him.

"Now that I've met all of you, I want to tell you what a pleasure it has been to watch you since you've been here. It has been a real joy. You are a crazy bunch, aren't you?" he jokes.

The contestants all giggle and laugh and I force myself to follow suit.

You're supposed to be happy to be here, I say to myself. Act accordingly.

"Well, good," he says. "I'm glad you're having a good time. That's what York is all about, after all."

Hardly, I say to myself.

"Now that we have all met, I want to announce to you, officially, whose hand in marriage you will be competing for."

The women around me look at him in anticipation.

I clench my jaw to keep my heart from jumping out of my chest.

The King waits for a moment and then a big eager smile spreads across his face.

"Me!" he announces proudly.

CHAPTER 11 - EVERLY

WHEN WE SEE HIM...

The forced smile on my face vanishes immediately and I can't bring it back no matter what I do. Instead, I try to hide. I put my hand over my mouth and look surprised. The surprise is more of a shock and this is the only expression that's authentic.

So, at the end of this, if I beat out all the rest - and that's a big if - my prize will be marriage to *this* man?

I look at him as he watches our reaction.

There is ruthlessness in his eyes.

He knows everything about this place - all of its darkest corners and alcoves. But worse yet, he likes it that way.

After a few moments, I gather my thoughts and

paint a plastic smile on my face. Then I glance around the room at the other contestants.

Most are smiling and nodding just like they were before.

Did they know about this already?

Am I the only one who didn't? I look at Savannah and Olivia.

They are harder to read.

Their smiles are smaller, somewhat polite. Their grins aren't quite as wide-toothed in comparison to the others.

But what does that mean?

"I am pleased to see how excited you all are," the King says, nodding his head.

I narrow my eyes and try to analyze him. But what exactly am I looking for?

He's a man with immense wealth and power on the global stage. He's the head of a large company, probably even a conglomerate.

And yet, that's not enough for his ego.

He went out of his way to build up this island, create this place called York, which he rules as the King.

All titles have to be bequeathed with power. I can call myself the President of the United States all I want, but unless I'm elected and others approve of that title, it's meaningless.

But the fact that others refer to him as the King... my throat clenches up in fear.

The truth is that I know very, very little about this place and the people who run it. That's what happens when you are just a pawn in the game of chess.

You are nobody.

You are dispensable.

And yet, you do possess some power.

If you make it far enough, you can get a promotion.

A pawn has the ability to become a knight, rook, bishop, and queen.

My intention is to become Queen.

THE KING and Mirabelle exchange looks and she gives him a brief nod.

"Now, it's time for another introduction," the King says.

Two servers quickly walk over to the main doors and swing them open.

By now, I should expect the unexpected, but I do not expect to see him.

Easton.

I hate everything about this place, but *he* is the one I truly despise.

He made me believe that I might have a friend here.

He made me let down my guard.

He lied to me about his vulnerability.

All of that is unforgivable.

But he did teach me a valuable lesson; I cannot trust anyone here.

No matter what.

Dressed in an exquisite suit with French cuffs and sparkling cufflinks, which I'm sure are diamonds, he comes through the doors and takes his position next to his father.

Easton's face is calm and severe.

Unreadable.

His eyes refuse to meet mine.

The King proudly watches the contestants look at his son.

How much of what Easton told me was true? Does he really live in New York?

Does he really only come here for these events?

Or is everything I know about him a falsehood?

"Ladies, this is my son, Easton Bay," the King says.

My eyes dart to Mirabelle. Her one foot steps behind the other in a curtsy.

I quickly follow suit. When I return back up, I'm startled to see the King's eyes on mine. He gives me an approving nod.

Easton takes a step forward and proceeds to give each of us a kiss on the back of the hand.

When he comes to me, my whole body starts to shake. But I try to keep myself composed.

You can do this, I say to myself over and over.

Easton takes a step toward me and, for the first time since he has been in this room, our eyes meet. His are dark and as mysterious as ever.

His face is expressionless, calm; it's what I imagine a sociopath looks like.

I cannot read it like Abbott's face.

It doesn't flash in anger, disappointment, or any other emotion.

He is stoic and reserved.

"It is a pleasure to see you again, Ms. March," Easton says and kisses the back of my hand. I flutter my eyelashes at him and nod.

"The pleasure is all mine," I lie.

"Ah, ah, ah, Easton," the King says. "Now, are you supposed to call her that?"

Easton looks at him without a tinge of fear.

"I figured we could let go of the formalities now that she and I have been better acquainted?"

The King narrows his eyes in disapproval.

"Oh, I'm sorry, was I not supposed to share that information?" Easton challenges him. What is going on here? I wonder. Why is he doing this?

"Well, if you want to do away with the formalities, let's!" the King announces. "No more numbers, ladies. From now on, you may go by your real names."

The King doesn't seem pleased to be forced into this position, but he doesn't explain himself further.

I look up at Easton, confused. He doesn't give me a response.

What I do realize is that he has put me into a precarious position.

Now I'm going to have to explain myself to Olivia, Savannah, and everyone else.

Why did Easton call me Ms. March?

What does he know about me?

And what should I say in return?

"Since you are already acquainted with Ms. March, why not meet the rest of the ladies?" the

King suggests. Easton clenches his jaw, but keeps his thoughts to himself.

"Go on now," the King nudges.

Easton takes a deep breath and does as he is told. Each contestant gives him her name and he again kisses their hand and tells them what a pleasure it is to meet them. When it's my turn, he skips over me and goes straight to Olivia.

"Perfect," the King says after Easton takes a step back from the last one on the end.

CHAPTER 12 - EVERLY

WHEN THERE'S AN ANNOUNCEMENT...

*T*he King is toying with him.
Mocking him.

There's tension between them, and that tension makes me wonder.

How complicit was Easton in what he did back there? When he seduced me?

"Okay then, now that you have all met, I have an announcement to make," he says. "Your challenge."

The women all gasp and a few even clap from excitement. I continue to stand there with a blank expression and an unwavering smile on my face.

"Your challenge will be a simple one. You see this man here?" he says, pointing to Easton. "You will have to go on a date with him."

Easton's face remains expressionless and I have

no idea if this is news to him or not. The girls, on the other hand, get excited. They clap and cheer and one of them even jumps up and down.

I can't bring myself to feign that level of exuberance.

"So, what about you, Ms. March?" the King calls me out. "Everyone seems very happy with this news. How about you?"

I shrug before I can stop myself.

"I'm pleased, your majesty," I say.

"You don't look pleased."

"It's just that I'm wondering why the task is to go on a date with your son when we are in competition to marry you?"

The words just come out of my mouth before I can stop myself.

Shut up, Everly, I say to myself. Just shut up.

"Well, since you asked... I trust my son. He has a good head on his shoulders and I want to see you all on a date. But maybe because I have other things to do at this point."

He doesn't need to offer me this explanation, of course.

I mean, who the hell am I here? But he does and I appreciate it. Even though I doubt that it's the truth.

"I appreciate your explanation," I say graciously. "Thank you."

"Okay, then." The King claps his hands. "I will be retiring for the night. So, I bid you farewell."

The servers open the doors for him and he leaves. Easton quickly exits behind him.

"So?" Olivia turns to me as soon as they both leave. "What happened? You already know Easton?"

Her eyes glisten with excitement. She's holding my hands in the air in front of hers in anticipation.

"It's nothing," I mumble.

"Oh, c'mon! Don't lie to me, girl!" she says.

"Yes, tell us. What's the deal?" Savannah asks.

The rest of the contestants, the girls I have yet to meet, gather around me. I'm on the spot. I want to tell them the truth, but I don't know if I should.

"Nothing." I shrug. "It's really nothing."

"Oh, c'mon, it has to be something," Olivia presses.

I know that I won't be able to get away with just saying nothing.

"Well, if you must know," I say, leaning closer to them. "I met him before. In the garden. He was just sitting there and we started talking. I had no idea who he was. That's why I was so surprised when he came in here."

CHARLOTTE BYRD

"So, you didn't know he was the prince?"

I shake my head no and try to look as innocent as possible. I must be getting better at this lying thing because they all smile and nod at me, waiting for my next lie.

"I had no idea," I say with a big shrug. "Honestly, if I had, I would've probably freaked out or something. He was just sitting and we got to talking. I told him my name, stuff like that."

"Did he tell you his?" Olivia asks.

It's a challenge. I think. But I'm not sure. I roll the dice.

"Yes, he did. Just his first name though."

"I can't believe you met the Prince," Savannah squeals. "And he's quite easy on the eyes, too."

"Yeah, I guess."

"You guess? Are you blind?" Olivia asks.

I laugh. "I was just joking. Of course, I know he's hot."

We continue to discuss the Prince's various virtues ad nauseam. It's not that I don't agree.

Yes, he's attractive.

Yes, he's dashing.

But I know a lot more about him and that sort of taints my overall picture.

74

* * *

AFTER A WHILE, Mirabelle returns and politely nudges us to retire for the night. I let out a big sigh of relief. Finally, I can get some sleep. I'm one of the first girls to climb the stairs. As soon as I get to my room, I immediately climb out of my clothes and let out an even bigger sigh of relief.

As I get into the shower to wash the night's festivities off me, my thoughts return to Paige. Oh, how I wish she hadn't reacted like she did back there. She does not deserve to be eliminated. Not for that.

Of course, that's not why they took her away. It was not the simple act of attacking that man that threatened them. It was the fact that her mere presence was a challenge to their way of life.

Paige had become unpredictable.

Volatile.

She stood up to them and they couldn't deal with it.

Tears start to run down my face. I didn't know her well, but I miss her terribly.

After I turn off the water, I wrap myself in a big puffy towel that goes all the way to down to the floor and I don't bother to towel myself off.

I walk straight to the bed and get under the covers.

How many more days of this can I handle?

My nervous system won't be able to manage it. I know that.

And yet, I don't have a choice.

I hate this place, but there's nothing I can do about it. I can't change my circumstances. All I can change is how I think about them.

And with that, I turn off the lights and close my eyes.

Tomorrow is another day.

I need to gather my strength to make it a good one.

CHAPTER 13 - EASTON

WHEN DARKNESS DESCENDS...

That look on her face.

It consumed me. Tormented me.

I could see the anguish through the facade of darkness.

Come back to me, Everly, I wanted to scream at the top of my lungs. Come back to me!

I need you to believe me.

I didn't do that for him.

I didn't do it just because of the order.

I did it to protect you.

Also, I did it because to touch you is to touch heaven.

As I stand before her with a stoic expression on my face and watch my father make a mockery of everything that is beautiful and kind, I try to remember the last time I felt this way toward someone.

Alicia understood a part of me.

She was there for me.

A good friend.

A lover.

A beautiful soul who deserved so much more than what I could offer her.

But the connection I feel toward Everly now...it's so much more than that.

After only a few days, I feel like she gets me. We don't have to speak. In fact, we can't. Not really.

And yet, I look into her eyes and it's like she understands. At least, that's what it felt like on those glorious days that she spent with me in my chambers.

And now, looking at her face, despite the blank expression that she has painted on it, I know that she feels pain. I know that she hates me.

She blames me.

She despises me.

But what can I do?

I go through the motions. I participate in my father's little show and dance and then leave. I've had enough of this place a long time ago.

I want to disappear.

Escape.

Never come back again.

But I can't.

Now, I'm invested.

Now, there's someone who I can't leave behind.

Even when I step outside the mansion's door, I can still sense her. She has put up a wall around herself to protect what's inside. If I ever want to connect with her again, I'll have to break through those walls.

Will I be able to?

Is it even worth trying?

I wander around in the moonlight. The palm trees lining the walkway sway in the breeze coming off the ocean. Some of them are bending so hard into the wind that they are practically lying down on the ground. But that's how they have to be to survive the hurricanes that slam into this place in the fall.

They have to be flexible and nimble.

The ones that aren't will break by the force that comes at them.

I know that's how I need to be as well.

In order to beat my father at his game, I need to learn how to play it well. But what does that mean exactly?

When I was younger, my father taught us to play

chess. It is his favorite game and he uses it as a type of litmus test, a way to gauge how intelligent someone is.

Naturally, as a kid, I was never very good at it. I mean, I could make some moves, play the game, but he would inevitably beat me.

And he always did.

Over and over again.

He never let me win.

Later, in therapy, I learned that he wouldn't let me win because of his ego. His ego was so fragile that he couldn't even pretend to lose to a child to build up my confidence and self-esteem.

At that time, however, he said that he would never let me lose to build up my character. That way, were I to ever beat him for real, then I would know that I had indeed beat him.

Well, I never did.

Not once.

After a while, we stopped playing entirely. He got bored and moved on to other character-building exercises.

He never let Abbott win either, but they stopped playing when Abbott lost his temper and punched a hole in the wall.

I'm not sure what this says about me.

Perhaps, it just says that I'm not very good at chess.

But life isn't really chess, is it? People who like to play chess think so, but where would we be if there were only chess players in the world?

Even though I never beat him at chess, I do have to beat him at this. Or die trying.

SUDDENLY, I hear a familiar voice coming from the other side of the pool, just past the grotto. I duck behind one of the thicker trees. My father is talking to one of his oldest advisors.

I know him only as Dagger and he has been in my father's employ since the founding of the House of York.

Dagger is a tall snake of a man with sharp eyebrows and a long tongue, which he uses every opportunity to show off.

I can't quite make out what they are saying until my father says, "Let me know if Easton starts to fall for that March girl. I like her."

"Yes, I can see that," Dagger says. "You've gone out of your way to protect her on a number of occasions."

"She has spunk; you don't see that much nowadays."

Their conversation about Everly makes my skin crawl.

"And of course, I wouldn't want the same thing to happen to her as what happened to that little bitch who was going to run away with him," my father says with a loud bellowing laugh.

What? What did he say? Did I hear that correctly?

I shake my head in disbelief.

My throat seizes up.

The blood in my body seems to stop circulating and my hands get clammy.

Dagger laughs. "Don't even mention her. You don't know how hard it was to get to her and lock her down there while keeping him away. They were quite inseparable, as you remember."

"I know, I know," my father says, waving his hand. "You are a master."

"I've been your loyal subject for a long time."

"Loyal friend," my father corrects him. "You know, Dagger, you need a wife. And children. I can't tell you how much fun they bring into your life, especially if you aren't the one taking care of them."

"I'll work on it, sir."

PART 3

CHAPTER 14 - EASTON

WHEN I SEE RED...

I stand stunned by what I just heard.

Father and Dagger walk away laughing, but I don't follow them.

My head is spinning out of control.

How could he do that to me?

He knew how much I loved her.

He knew that we were planning on starting our life together and he just swept in and took it all away from me.

He took *her* away from me.

My father killed Alicia.

The thought seems foreign and strange. I've had my suspicions, of course. I've had plenty of those.

He made derogatory comments about her. He

made his jokes. He tried to get me to break up with her.

First, by trying to manipulate me.

Then by spreading lies about her.

And finally, just by putting in an order.

Dagger was the one who actually did it.

But how?

My thoughts return to that day.

We thought our departure was a secret.

We thought that no one would know.

We thought that we could just sneak out at night and sail away from everyone and everything. But *someone* knew.

I was running away because I hated Father's hatred. I hated everything he stood for and I needed to start my life away from him.

But he couldn't let me go.

He could've just let me disappear.

He could've just pretended that he didn't know. But he didn't.

My father hates everything about me, yet he wants me around.

A few years ago, I went to a shrink to talk about this because I felt like I was suffocating with each breath. After a few sessions, he told me that my father wants me around because he wants to control me.

He wants to control everything about my life. I didn't believe him at the time. Back then, I thought that my father still had a shred of love or affection toward me.

But now I know that he was right.

The fact that I loved Alicia didn't matter to him.

She was taking me away from him and he couldn't have it. She had to go.

Of course, it had to be an accident. She was the daughter of a very important person in his company.

There were appearances to keep up.

I clench my fists. My head starts to throb, as if these thoughts are physical things that are running into the walls of my brain.

The pit of my stomach fills with anger and hate.

I lust for revenge.

He will pay for what he did to her.

They both will, I promise myself. How? I don't know yet.

A part of me wants to do it quickly.

I'm not Abbott. I don't respond immediately with anger.

But on this occasion, it takes actual restraint to

stop myself from following Dagger and just stabbing him to death.

He's the one who actually killed Alicia.

But what about my father? If I act now, without a plan, I will only be able to get one of them.

That's not good enough.

That's *nowhere near* good enough.

And if I do get Dagger? What will happen then?

I won't be able to get off this island without getting caught. Not without a plan.

And if I do get caught, what then? A trial? A guilty verdict for killing one of the King's men.

A death sentence for treason, or maybe worse; a lifetime in prison?

And what about my father?

He was the one who ordered the murder. Does he just get away with everything forever?

I imagine going to my father's chambers and attacking him. I imagine my hands wrapping tightly around his throat, squeezing the life out of him.

I imagine the way his eyes would bug out of his skull and him pleading for his life.

I want that. Oh, how I want that.

But a quick death like that isn't good enough for the King of York.

Oh, no.

The King of York needs to suffer.

And he will suffer most by losing everything that he has built.

To properly avenge him and all of his sins, the King of York needs to lose his whole fortune and then his title and this place he calls home.

He needs to see his life's work go up in flames.

And then, and only then, will I end his life.

How does that line go again?

Revenge is a dish best served cold.

Cold because it needs to be planned.

Cold because it cannot be over in a moment.

Just taking their lives isn't enough.

Alicia deserves so much more.

She deserves the destruction of a place that forces women to do things against their will.

It will not be easy and it will not be quick.

But nothing worth doing is.

It is effort and determination, which make the most daring of dreams a reality. It is effort and determination and, hopefully, a bit of luck which will give me my revenge.

The rage and anger that consumed me only a minute ago seems to dissipate.

Suddenly, my life has a purpose.

A goal.

My father wanted to keep me from running away from York.

My father wanted to keep me from pretending that this place didn't exist.

Well, he is getting what he wants.

I will no longer close my eyes to the realities of this place.

From now on, my life's only purpose will be to work toward destroying everything that Alistair Bay built and everything that he is.

CHAPTER 15 - EASTON

WHEN I GO THROUGH THE MOTIONS...

*O*ver the next few days, I fulfill my duties as a loyal son.

I go on a bunch of dates and act cordial and polite.

We go out to dinner, eating by the ocean, and talk about who we are.

Well, mainly I ask about them. I focus my attention on them so that I don't have talk too much about myself.

They are only too happy to oblige.

They go into their backgrounds and their life stories.

I only half listen.

None of them seem to notice.

I keep waiting for the one person I do want to

have a date with. But the closer I get to seeing Everly, the more nervous I get.

"So, what made you want to come here and participate in this?" I ask the girl named Olivia. She's easy on the eyes and knows how to carry herself. She easily moves among different topics of conversation, jumping from literature, to art, to history.

"It sounded exciting. I'm single so I thought, why not?" she says, kicking her foot under the table toward mine. I force a smile.

"Are you okay?" she asks after a moment.

"Yes, of course." I try to snap out of it.

"Because you seem sort of...distant."

I shrug. You caught me.

"I hope it's not anything I said."

I reassure her that it's not, but I'm not too convincing.

"You know if you don't want to be on this date with me, you don't have to be," she says, taking her napkin from her lap.

I'm caught a little off-guard.

She rises from behind the table and starts to walk away. "Olivia, wait!" I yell after her.

In a few steps, I catch up with her.

"Where are you going?"

"Home."

"Why?"

"I told you. I don't need you to do me any favors. If you don't want to go on a date with me, you don't have to."

"That's not exactly how it works here."

"I don't care," she says, folding her hands across her chest. "That's how it works with me."

She's right.

I shouldn't be rude.

It's just that she's my eighth date in a row.

"I'm sorry, I'm just a bit...tired."

"Are you?" She challenges me. "Or are you just looking forward to seeing Everly?"

I take a step back. "What do you mean?"

"You knew her from before. She said she met you in the garden and that you didn't tell her who you really were."

I nod.

"Is that true?"

"Yes, of course."

"Doesn't sound like it." She narrows her eyes.

She gives me a look like she can see right through me.

"What do you mean?" I ask tentatively.

"I have a feeling that she knows you a lot better than she would after just one meeting."

I shrug and deny it vehemently. If that's what she told them, then I have to keep to her story. There should be no reason for her to lie.

"I don't know what you want from me, Olivia," I say coldly, looking straight into her eyes. "I told you already. I'm tired. I have been on a lot of dates. I'm not exactly used to this."

She shrugs.

"If you don't believe me, that's fine. Don't. Let's end the date right now."

Without another word, she spins on her heels and walks away.

Well, that went well, I say to myself sarcastically. I can't help but like her spunk. If I were indeed making recommendations to my father about a girl that he would like spending time with, she would definitely be on top of the list.

THE DATES ARE STACKED two or three throughout the day, and my date with Everly is at the end of the third day. Right after my fight with Olivia.

The only reason I didn't protest the other dates is that I wanted my alone time with Everly. The time is finally here and I'm so nervous my heart feels like it's about to jump out of my chest.

Everly comes downstairs in a short cocktail dress. Her hair cascades down her shoulders and her eyes twinkle under the soft light of the chandelier.

She looks even more beautiful than I remember.

I hand her the roses that I brought for her, just like I did for all the other contestants. The roses are a requirement.

She thanks me for them politely and I escort her out of the door.

As we walk toward the place where they will be serving us dinner, we make a little bit of small talk.

Nothing significant.

Just an exchange of pleasantries.

Something I can't stand.

But I go through the motions because she does and because everyone is watching.

Much to my dismay, dinner proceeds just like it did with the other contestants. We discuss the items on the menu. She offers a few tidbits of why she prefers some foods to others. Whether these are in fact true, I have no idea.

"Would you like to see our dessert menu?" the waiter asks after we finish.

"No," I say categorically. The waiter turns to Everly.

"No, she doesn't either," I speak for her. She looks at me inquisitively.

"Not a fan of dessert?" she asks.

I shake my head. "Not really," I add.

I try to speak to her without saying a word. But we don't know each other well enough for that. Not yet.

I don't have to pay because this isn't a real restaurant. It's part of the show.

The event. The competition.

When I stand up, I give her my hand and help her out of the chair. She tries to pull her hand away from mine, but I don't let go. Instead, I reassert my grip and pull her closer to me.

"Where are we going?" she asks.

"Somewhere private."

CHAPTER 16 - EVERLY

WHEN WE GO SOMEWHERE MORE PRIVATE...

When he takes my hand, sparks rush through my body. He leads me down a narrow path through the trees toward the sand. The conversation at dinner was cold and sterile. I was polite, but not forthcoming. I answered his questions, but rarely asked any in return. I don't trust him and I'm not going to pretend I do. It is all just an act anyway, on his part. Right?

My heels sink into the sand and I find it difficult to walk.

"Take off your shoes," he says.

"Why?"

"Please?"

I narrow my eyes but do as he says. The sand isn't very good for them anyway.

Easton grabs my hand again and asks, "Do you trust me?"

"No."

"I don't think you can do it with them on," he says.

"Do what?"

"Run!" Easton whispers loudly, pulling me forward.

There isn't menace in his voice and I'm not afraid of him. But I slow down after a few moments and pull my hand away from him.

"What are you doing?" I demand to know. "Where are we going?"

"I can't tell you."

"Well, I'm not going then," I say, crossing my arms across my chest. "I've had enough of your lies, Easton."

Inhaling deeply, his nostrils flare a bit.

"We're going somewhere private. I can't tell you because then...it will be easier for them to find out." He says the last bit in a very hushed tone. Barely audible. Especially over the crashing of the waves and whistle of the breeze coming off the ocean.

"What? I don't understand."

"They're watching us...But...I need to talk to

you... I need to explain everything," he whispers again.

His lips are barely moving and it takes me a minute to piece together exactly what he is saying.

My body responds with a nod even before I have a moment to really process it. And with that nod, he takes my hand in his and we begin to run again.

The wind seems to come from all directions. It whips my hair around so much that I can barely see anything in front of my face. I keep putting one foot in front of the other, holding on tightly to Easton's hand.

The white sand looks black in the moonlight, and it feels cool between my feet. We run on the part right by the water to avoid sinking too much into the sand, and the warm Caribbean water occasionally comes up and sweeps over my feet.

The waves foam a little when they crash, but they are small and hardly visible. The ocean here is calm and peaceful, which is more than what can be said for the land.

Somewhere around where the land makes a little bend, Easton turns away from the water. The sand gets deeper and deeper, caking onto my wet feet.

"Where are we going?" I ask, trying to catch my breath.

The sand is uneven and unstable, swaying my body from side to side as I half walk, half run behind him.

"We're almost there," he says, tugging me forward.

His breathing isn't forced at all or difficult, and he seems to have barely broken a sweat. On the other hand, I am drenched. I'm perspiring so much that the droplets from my forehead are even sliding into my eyes, burning my corneas.

I wipe my forehead with the back of my hand and one foot gets tangled up with the other. A moment later, I slip and fall right into the sand.

"Are you okay?" Easton immediately kneels down toward me.

"Um, yeah," I mumble.

I try to get up without getting even more sandy, but that's nearly impossible. The sand is as fine as powdered sugar and it adheres to every inch of my skin that it comes in contact with. Trying to brush it off with my other hand just makes things worse.

"C'mon, we're almost there. I'll help you get this off when we get inside," he whispers.

"Inside where?" I ask, but he ignores me.

Instead, he takes me by my arm to help me along.

A few minutes later, we walk into the mouth of a large cave.

It's pitch black inside.

Easton pulls out three candles from his pocket and lights them.

The candles illuminate the large concave sides of the cave and a bit of the tunnel leading into the darkness.

The cave is wet with humidity and smells of the sea. The air here is thick and when I open my mouth, all I taste is salt.

"Here, let me help you," Easton says.

He starts with my left arm and uses quick motions to brush off the sand. When he gets to my chest, he carefully avoids my breasts and then moves up to my face.

Pulling my hair out of the way, Easton runs his fingers through it. Then he sweeps his fingers across my left cheek.

He's careful and meticulous.

Professional, even.

Watching him work, I suddenly have an urge in the pit of my stomach.

I glance up at his luscious lips and the way the candlelight cradles his strong jaw.

I want him.

Easton continues to work. When he gets to my eyes, he presses his fingertips into my skin to get the grains to stick to him instead. He slowly makes his way around my face and down my neck, carefully removing all the sand.

"I think this is as good as I can get it for now," Easton says after a few moments.

"Thank you, I appreciate it," I whisper.

We stand here locked in each other's gaze, unable to move. But then he takes a step back.

"I needed to talk to you in private," Easton says.

I nod.

"My father ordered me to sleep with you to teach *me* some sort of lesson. And I couldn't say no," he says.

His voice starts out calm, but quickly gets frantic.

"They were going to eliminate you if I didn't do it. And I couldn't let that happen, Everly. I couldn't let them send you away from here to some horrible place where they'd do who knows what to you."

"That's so unlike this place," I say sarcastically.

"I know, I know. York is...terrible. But it's the devil I know. So that's what I chose."

I shrug.

"Do you want to be eliminated?" he asks.

"I don't want to marry your father."

Easton takes a deep breath. "That's not going to happen."

"Yeah, right," I say. "That's going to happen but only if I'm extremely lucky. The chances are I'm still going to be eliminated, Easton."

"I wanted to buy you some time."

"Why?"

"Because I care about you," he says.

"I don't believe you," I lie.

"I care about you a lot more than I should." He ignores me.

"I don't believe you," I say again, but this time the words come out a little fractured and a lot less convincing.

"Caring is a weakness here. It's something that they can use against me. But I can't help how I feel."

WHEN WE ARE ALONE...

I don't want to believe him.

He's a liar.

A traitor.

He tricked me into sleeping with him.

I want to believe all of these things, but I don't.

I can't.

They don't feel right.

The thing that does feel right is that Easton's telling me the truth.

"So... in this cave, they can't hear us?" I ask.

He shakes his head no.

"Will they be able to find us?"

"Yes. There are footprints leading them here. They will be here soon."

"What are you going to say when they come?" I ask.

"That I wanted some alone time with you. That we went on a walk and got lost."

"They won't believe you," I say.

"I know, but what else can I do? I needed to talk to you. Frankly."

I nod and look down at the ground.

"Do you believe me, Everly?"

I shrug.

I don't want to admit it out loud.

Not yet.

He lifts my chin toward his.

"You have to believe me," he whispers.

"And if I don't?"

He darts his eyes away from me.

"Actually, it's probably for the best. If you don't believe me, then it's fine. I just wanted to tell you anyway."

Easton turns to face away from me. His shoulders slope down and he sits down on the large boulder by the other side of the cave.

"Why are you here?" I ask. "You are so much better than this place."

He inhales deeply.

"Why don't you just run away and disappear? Never come back?"

He looks up at me.

His dark eyes narrow and the expression on his face changes from forlorn to severe. He purses his lips and clenches his jaw.

"I tried to do that before with Alicia," he says, looking straight at me.

Loose strands of hair fall into his face and he brushes them away with the back of his hand.

"Can I tell you something in confidence?" he asks.

I narrow my eyes and nod. He takes a deep breath.

"They killed her," he says after a moment.

"What?" I ask, shaking my head.

"I had my suspicions about it, but then I heard them talking. Somehow, they found out about our plan to run away together and they staged the fire and sank the boat. They locked her downstairs and I couldn't get her out."

As he talks, his voice cracks in parts.

Tears well up in the bottom of his eyes, but his fists clench up. It's as if he's teetering between anger and sorrow.

I walk over to him and take a seat next to him.

"I shouldn't be telling you this," he says, hanging his head. I put my arm around his shoulders.

"You don't have to," I mumble.

"My father ordered the kill," he continues. "I heard him joking about it. He said that she was getting in the way. But they had to make it look like an accident because she was the daughter of a family friend."

I don't know what else to say except that I'm sorry. We sit in silence for a few moments.

"My father is a very dangerous man," Easton says. "But I have been afraid of him long enough."

The determination in his voice startles me.

"What are you going to do?" I ask.

"I don't know yet, but I'm going to avenge her death. She didn't deserve it. He killed her just to get me to stay."

"Your father has done a lot of terrible things," I mumble.

We hear voices out in the distance.

They are coming.

My heart drops.

Easton turns toward me and takes my face into his hands. He looks straight into my eyes.

"I will do everything in my power to protect you,"

he says. "Everything I do will be to make sure that no harm will come to you."

He presses his lips onto mine.

They are soft and effervescent.

As my mouth opens up to welcome his, I taste his intensity and determination. But there's something else in the kiss as well.

A bit of kindness.

A bit of human decency.

All the things that I had forgotten about since I've been here in York.

I close my eyes and kiss him back.

Easton buries his hands in my hair. He tugs slightly, pulling my head back. Then his mouth leaves my lips and goes down my neck.

Shivers run up my arms as he buries his face in my breasts. His movements gather momentum.

They seem to take on a life of their own. It's not just his movements, but ours together.

Our hands intertwine and our fingers become one.

My hair becomes his hair.

My lips become his lips.

Somewhere in the distance, I hear people's voices. They are getting louder. Closer.

"They're coming," I whisper while our lips are still interlocked.

"I know," he says and wraps his arms around me tighter.

"What should we do?"

"Keep kissing."

I don't know if that's the right thing or not, but I don't argue.

Instead, I let go.

I lose myself in his mouth, his body, and his passion.

This moment will not last, but I can make it last as long as possible.

Maybe then it can sustain me on the dark nights to come.

"I am falling in love with you, Everly," Easton says.

His words come out deep and almost threatening in tone.

He gives me one last tug on my hair, kissing near the bottom of my neck near my collarbone.

A warm sensation starts to build in between my legs. I haven't felt this aroused since the last time we were together.

I run my fingers down his hard body, enjoying the feel of each isolated muscle.

My hand lands in between his legs and I grab onto him, remembering how good it made me feel not so long ago.

His mouth returns to mine and I lose myself completely.

Suddenly, a flash of light blinds me.

They are here.

CHAPTER 18 - EVERLY

WHEN THEY FIND US...

*A*s I pull away from Easton, I wonder what's going to happen now.

Will the guards pull me away and throw me in the dungeon again?

Will I be eliminated?

Will I be sent away to some foreign land that will make this place seem like paradise?

As these questions pop into my head, another feeling gnaws at me. None of that would be as bad as never seeing Easton again.

As I stand next to him, holding his hand, I intertwine my fingers with his.

My heart is pounding a mile a minute. It feels like it's about to jump out of my chest.

When I look up at him, I see spots from the flood of light, but I can still somewhat make out his face.

He clenches his jaw and looks straight ahead.

It's as if he's challenging anyone out there to come for me. To force me away from him.

We wait.

Time seems to pass into infinity. It's so quiet that all I hear is the sound of little water droplets landing on the floor of the cave after making their long trip from the ceiling.

I can't see anything looking straight on, so I look up instead.

The ceiling is textured with different size formations hanging down from it. What are they called again? My thoughts go back to eighth grade Earth Science with Mr. Box, the man with a 70's porn star mustache and an unwavering enthusiasm for science.

Yes, of course!

Stalactites hang from the ceiling of a cave while stalagmites grow from the cave floor.

As my eyes adjust to the light, I see that this one doesn't have too many stalagmites on the floor in the center where we are, but it does have a bunch further down into the tunnel.

All of these thoughts occur to me in a matter of moments.

That's what it's like when you are waiting for the unknown.

But then, someone points the light down and darkness descends around us.

"This is highly irregular."

The words are delivered in a very disapproving tone and they come from the silhouette of a short, pudgy man with a comb-over. As my eyes try to adjust, my vision is flooded with spots.

"Mr. Bay? Aren't you going to say anything?"

"I don't see why I need to," Easton says confidently. "I am on a date, right?"

The man doesn't respond.

"Am I on a date?" Easton asks.

What is he getting at? I wonder.

"Yes."

Easton shrugs as if the answer is clear. I look around and it's not clear to anyone else but me.

"What does that mean, Mr. Bay?"

"Listen, Belding. I don't need to explain myself to you."

"But I'm the event planner."

"Exactly!" Easton takes my hand and leads me

out of the cave, past all the people with huge flashlights.

"Mr. Bay!" Belding runs after us, tripping in the sand.

"What?" Easton asks.

"I don't understand what's going on. You should've stayed at the restaurant."

"I was bored at the restaurant. I've been on what feels like a million dates this week and I wanted a change. I want to make a real connection. I mean, I am on a date, right?"

Belding shrugs. I notice that he has a significant bald spot on the back of his head, which he tries to cover up with hair from around it.

"All dates and interactions must be recorded," Belding says after a moment.

Easton just waves his hand and pulls me away from him toward the beach. Belding catches up to us.

"Mr. Bay, I can get fired for this. Your father..." His voice trembles when he brings him up.

"Don't worry about my father. He's my problem. Besides, I'm not lying to you. I got tired of the boring sit down dates and I wanted to get to know her a little more. Isn't that the point of this competition? Isn't that what I'm doing for my father?"

Belding shrugs, unable to figure out what to say in response.

"I just don't want to get in trouble for this," he finally says quietly.

I inhale deeply.

The fear instilled by that man into everyone here, not just the captives, but practically everyone who works for him, is astonishing.

I used to think that everyone was conspiring against us.

I used to think that they were all being paid off to be here, but now I know that's not true.

They may be paid, but they are also afraid.

Terrified.

Scared-shitless of the King of York.

This realization makes my heart heavy and tired. People who are paid off can be swayed with money.

Not that I have any, but they could be swayed by being discovered or found out somehow.

But what about people who are afraid? Like abused animals, they only know how to lash out.

They have trouble trusting because their trust has been violated for so long.

My trust was violated, too. But I wasn't here that long.

I haven't made my whole life on York and I still

have plenty of memories of how things should be to keep me going.

But what about Belding? And Mirabelle and all the rest of them?

Their life is here and they live behind those walls.

They don't know any other way to be.

We walk back into the restaurant where the lights are bright and the cameras in the ceiling are rolling.

I take Easton's hand in mine and say, "I had a wonderful time."

I stand up on my tiptoes and press my lips to his.

He immediately reciprocates, taking me into his arms.

His lips burn mine as he buries his hands in my hair.

For a brief moment, we push the outside world away.

For a brief moment, there's no one else around but us.

CHAPTER 19 - EASTON

WHEN WE COME BACK...

*W*hy did I kiss her back there in the cave when I knew they were coming?

Fuck them, that's why.

Because I wanted to.

Because I needed to.

Those are great answers, but I'm not so foolhardy.

Yes, I wanted to have her.

Yes, I needed to taste her.

But I also wanted another thing.

They were going to suspect something anyway if they found us in the cave.

So, why not just show them? Why not show a

beautiful romantic date that ended in a kiss? That's the goal of any successful date, isn't it?

So, when Everly thought about pulling away, I just kept kissing her harder. They would be here at any moment, I thought.

They would see us.

They would stand in awe in catching us doing something like that. And that's exactly what I wanted. Then something occurs to me.

Is that why Everly kissed me again?

Just now?

I stand next to her and lose myself in her.

Her taste.

Her smell.

The texture of her hair.

The little pieces of sand that I feel at the edges of my fingertips.

I want her.

All of her.

Right now.

I want this moment to last as long as possible and so does she.

So, what begins as an act of defiance, something for show, becomes something so much more than that.

Suddenly, we are lost in each other the way that we were all those days ago in my bed.

Wanting.

Craving.

Yearning.

Nothing else matters. No one else matters.

"Um, excuse me," Belding says after clearing his throat.

No one matters, least of all him.

Belding is his usual sniveling-bastard self. He acts as if he is afraid of my father when he is the first person to volunteer for every horrible thing that my father suggests. He is the worst example of a yes-man.

We pull away from each other, but keep our hands intertwined.

"Well, thank you for that, I guess," Belding says under his breath.

"Isn't that what you wanted to see?" Everly asks with the kind of confidence in her voice that I don't remember her exhibiting before, especially with the staff.

"What do you mean?" Belding asks, looking appalled.

"Well, you were complaining that what we did in

the cave wasn't captured for everyone, whoever they are, to see. So, here you are. We did it again."

I smile and give her a little squeeze of the hand.

"Well, you....still...shouldn't have...run away," Belding mumbles, tripping over his words.

"We wanted some privacy. You know, to have an authentic moment. You have seen what we have done there. Now, do you want to know what we talked about?"

My heart skips a beat. Everly's newfound confidence is making her push the boundaries.

Be quiet, I want to say, but I can't.

Probably feeling like he has been boxed in, Belding gives her a slight nod.

"We talked about this competition. Mainly, how unusual is it of the King to ask us, the women he is courting, to go out on a date with his son."

There it is.

My jaw nearly drops open.

The perfect response delivered perfectly.

Of course, this is something that people would talk about. It's so obvious and yet, only somewhat insulting.

But knowing what I know about my father, he likes a woman who's a bit of a challenge. He likes someone with a good strong head on her shoulders

119

and who isn't afraid to speak her mind, even though by all accounts she should keep her mouth shut.

"Wouldn't you agree?" Everly presses.

"With what?"

"With the fact that it's unusual?"

"No, I wouldn't say that," Belding says.

I don't expect any other answer, but I am still surprised just how brown-nosing he can be.

"Really? You oversee these type of competitions often?" Everly asks.

I can't help but smile.

"I know that the King has his reasons for doing what he's doing," Belding says after a long thought.

He thinks he's so clever and loyal.

Well, I guess he is loyal.

And with that, Everly drops the matter.

Like an expert diplomat, she doesn't push for more than what she wants. She had dropped him to his knees, metaphorically speaking, and that's where she will leave him.

"If you don't mind, I'm going to escort my date to her room now," I say and we walk away.

Everly and I walk away hand in hand.

We don't say much as I walk her back inside her house and up the stairs to her room. None of the other contestants are around as they are forbidden from leaving their rooms and being in any common areas while one of them is on a date.

The purpose of this is, of course, to create the illusion of privacy. That pretty much sums up everything about York in a nutshell.

Even though all eyes are on us just like they were at the beginning of the date, the walk to her room feels completely different.

We made a connection, one that will not be easy to break.

As I look into her eyes, I do not feel any regret in telling her what I found about my father and Alicia.

She will not betray me.

Of this, I am certain.

As I take her face into my hands, there are so many more things that I want to tell her.

In a world built on lies, it is remarkable to find a person with whom I can share my truth.

But alas, I cannot.

There is one thing that I can do.

I can give her another kiss.

I press my lips onto hers and wait for her mouth to open. I wrap my arms around her waist and for a few moments, the outside world falls away and disappears. Too bad that it has to be heard from again.

CHAPTER 20 - EASTON

WHEN I SEE HIM...

I walk down the stairs with a heavy heart. I miss her.

I want to run back to her room and spend the night with her, but the date is over and there are certain appearances to uphold.

I've already shown her too much preference as is. I don't want to make my feelings for her even more obvious.

When I walk out the back of the house, I pause for a moment to enjoy the soft breeze coming off the ocean. It tosses my hair from side to side, and it tastes of salt.

My thoughts keep returning to Everly.

Her eyes.

Her long neck.

Her perky breasts.

Her lean strong shoulders.

Her sharp tongue.

But I will go crazy thinking about her.

No, I need to put her out of my mind.

In front of me, the ocean spreads out into the darkness. The stars above illuminate just the ripples on top of the water slightly, but it's enough to call me inside.

I take off my shirt and walk briskly toward the water. When I get to the shore, I pull off the rest of my clothes and wade in.

The water is warm, just a few degrees cooler than the air. But it's refreshing anyway. When I get to about waist deep, I dive in. I hold my breath for as long as possible and just swim.

My feet make a large frog kick underneath while my arms follow along in a breast stroke. When I open my eyes a little, the salty water starts to burn.

The water around York is crystal clear.

During the days, you can see straight through the turquoise down to the yellow sandy floor.

But swimming through it at night, I don't see a thing except for the bubbles that escape from my mouth.

I come up for breath quickly, and then quickly

descend back down. This time, instead of swimming, I just allow myself to sink a little under water, watching hundreds of little bubbles, different sizes, escaping from my mouth.

They rush toward the surface, as if they were not made up of air, but were desperate to get air themselves.

As I swim, I feel all the tension in my body starting to dissipate.

My muscles start to relax and the world doesn't feel as heavy for a moment. It's all an illusion, of course. Because all that tension and uncertainty will be back as soon as I reach the surface. And it will multiply as soon as I get out of the water and feel the full weight of the gravitational pull on my body.

But, for now, well...I bend my knees and fall back under the water.

Sometime later, I climb out of the water and stand for a few minutes at the edge of the sand to air dry. The breeze feels a lot cooler now than it did before, but it stops short of being cold. When I'm sufficiently dry, I grab my clothes and shoes and walk back up the beach.

I don't want to put my clothes back onto my sticky flesh, but it would be inappropriate to walk all the way back to my house stark naked.

So, I compromise and just peel on my pants.

No underwear. No shoes. No shirt. Just the trousers.

Just as I get back up to the main level of the house, I see him.

A silhouette of a familiar man.

I have a good eye for faces, but he's facing away from me. I take a few quick steps forward and when he reaches for his bag to put into the back of the town car, my suspicions are confirmed.

"Jamie!" I yell and run up to him. He looks startled. His eyes grow big like sand dollars.

"Oh, hey," he mumbles and puts his other bag into the trunk.

The driver is sitting in the car, and I motion for him to wait.

"What are you doing here?" I ask.

"Leaving."

"Yes, I can see that. But what *were* you doing here?"

He glances up at me, clearly unwilling to answer any questions.

"Listen, I need to talk to you."

"I can't; my flight is leaving soon."

"Then you better talk fast."

He shakes his head. Openly defying me.

I take him by the collar. "Listen, you're going to talk to me either way. But we can have a nice chat or a bad one, it's up to you."

He gives me a nod.

I tell the driver that we will back in a few minutes and lead him back down to the beach for a bit of privacy. I don't know if anyone is watching, but I don't want to take any chances.

"Hey, man, what do you want?" Jamie asks, clearly irritated by all of this.

"What are you doing here?"

"I'm on a job. Just like I was in Philly. And Greenwich. And Boston. And Atlanta. What the fuck do you care?"

"What kind of job? Who hired you?"

Jamie drops his head. "I knew I should've never listened to him. What a bust."

I don't know what he's talking about, but I wait for him to continue.

"Listen, I don't know what the fuck is going on on this island, but I'm glad I'm getting off. It's definitely not worth the ten grand I was paid to bring those girls to those events."

"Really? Why is that?" I ask.

"Because...because...one little cunt attacked me! I mean, I was just there doing my job, working as a server of all things, and she just jumped up and fucking started cursing at me. And hit me really hard."

I resist the temptation to mock him. I want to ask if it were Everly? No, probably not since they would've eliminated her for that. Contestants were sent away for far less.

"So, you were working as a server here?" I press him.

"Yeah, can you believe that? What a joke."

I nod as if I agree or understand. I don't.

"How did you find out about this place?" I ask.

CHAPTER 21 - EASTON

WHEN I FIND OUT MORE...

Jamie shrugs his shoulders and looks at the ground.

"I was a broke grad student working at the Nantucket Country Club, trying to find a rich girl or a divorcee to take me away from my shitty life. And then my friend there told me about this job. Easy money. Doing supposedly super secret stuff for some billionaire. When they reached out to me, they said that this is what I'd have to do to start out. Basically, be a honey pot, you know? Meet some prospects they had their eyes on, ask them out, date them for a bit, and then invite them to this lavish party."

"Sounds like a good deal," I say to keep him talking.

"Yeah, I thought so, too. Only rule was that I couldn't sleep with them. No matter what. I didn't think they were really serious about that, but my friend Neil who came in the same time as me, lost his job for doing just that. They paid him anyway but he didn't get any more work."

"That sucks," I say.

"I know!" Jamie says, getting a bit more energized. I have the feeling that he has been keeping all of this inside long enough.

"But I have to tell you, that girl, Everly, you saw me with," Jamie says. I clench my fists until my knuckles turn white. "You remember Everly, right? You tried to stop her from getting into the cab with me?"

I shift my jaw around, but try to keep my cool. I hate the fact that he dares to mention her name at all. But punching him out and losing my cool isn't going to get me what I want. There's always time for that later.

"Yeah, I remember her."

"I really wanted to sleep with her, man," Jamie says, licking his lips like I'm one of the guys. "She had that body that's a little on the plump side, but also a bit of an attitude. I liked that. Out of all the dates that I brought to those Bay Foundation events, she was the one that I really wanted to bang."

Stay calm, Easton. Stay the fuck calm, I say to myself.

"So...your job was what exactly?" I push for more details.

This is the part of York that I know nothing about.

How do they find these women? There must be some sort of screening process, but what?

Jamie relaxes a bit and seems to forget that this is still an interrogation.

"Well, once I got hired, I got these encrypted emails. I had to put in all of these passwords and finally, I got their files. I can't remember the name of the first one I did. I remember following her for a bit and then seeing that she was a hostess at some five-star restaurant. So, I went over a few times. Sat at the bar and eventually started to make small talk. Then I laid on the compliments real thick. You know what I mean, right?"

I nod along as if I do to encourage him to keep talking, but inside I feel sick to my stomach.

Jamie tells me about reading through the girls' files and looking for weaknesses to exploit.

One was training to be a chef so he read up on food.

One was an elementary school teacher who liked hiking so suddenly he was an outdoor enthusiast.

He would become whatever the woman wanted him to be and then he would lead them to believe that they'd met someone really special.

After all their bad breakups and men who treated them shitty, they all thought that they had finally met the man of their dreams.

This was finally going to be a man who would respect them and engage with them, a man who didn't want to just get into their bed.

What they got instead was something much worse.

But there's something else that I don't quite understand.

"So what was the plan after you took them to that charity event?" I ask.

"Well, I'd get this text from the phone they provided. It would be either a thumbs up or thumbs down emoji."

"What did that mean?"

"Thumbs up emoji meant that it was a go. The girl was approved and I would slip something into her drink and invite her to my place. She would always pass out on the way and I would drive to a private airport and these other men would take her away from me. Then I would get my ten grand."

"Fuck," I whisper under my breath.

This is like some sort of spy shit, except that we're the bad guys.

"And if you got a thumbs down?" I ask. "What does that mean?"

"Nothing," Jamie says, shrugging. "That means that they didn't want her. So, I could take her home and she was free to go."

"So, you could sleep with them then?" I ask.

"Nope, still couldn't." He shakes his head, disappointed. "Not if I wanted to get paid the ten grand."

"So, you got paid either way?"

He nods in agreement.

"I got a bit of a bonus for knocking them out and driving them to the airport," he says. "Is that all? Can I go now?"

He starts to walk away, but I pull on his shirt and place him back in front of me.

"Fuck, what is it with this place!" he exclaims.

"It won't take too long," I say. "So, how is it that you ended up being a server here?"

"I just did. I did good bringing in those girls and

someone from the organization contacted me and said that they'd like to offer me a job here. On sight, he called it. I didn't realize that I would be fucking serving people."

"So, you just came here and you didn't know what you were going to do?"

"Hell no! I was a server in Nantucket. I had enough with serving rich people ridiculous food dressed in a tuxedo. I thought that I was going to do something fun. Something else. But that's where they put me. First in the kitchen as a dishwasher, and then in the front of the house. Well, fuck that."

I nod, taking it all in. He asks if he can go now and I give him a nod. I follow him back up to the car and watch as he opens the door.

"Hey!" Jamie yells back to me.

"What?" I take a few steps closer to him.

"That Everly girl from Philly," he says. Him saying her name makes my blood start to boil.

"What about her?"

"She must be one good fuck, huh?"

I slam my fist straight into the bridge of his nose.

One punch.

It's all it takes.

His head bobs back as if it's attached on a string.

A moment later, he's moaning and cradling his nose with his palms.

Blood splatters everywhere.

I nod to the driver to help get him inside the car.

When the door closes, I no longer hear the profanities that are pouring out of him.

CHAPTER 22 - EVERLY

WHEN WE CHAT...

The following morning after my date with Easton, all I want to do is to stay in bed and relax. But I can hear their voices downstairs and I know they're expecting a full blow by blow recap of everything that happened.

I wash my face, brush my hair and teeth. I put on some eyeliner and eyebrow tint as well as some mascara. I rarely wear foundation and typically concentrate all of my makeup on the eye region. I also hate the taste of anything on my lips at any time, let alone first thing in the morning, so I skip the lipstick.

The makeup isn't necessary, but I need it. It's armor. I'm wearing just enough to show that I care what I look like, but not enough that I would come off as someone who is trying too hard.

When I come downstairs, I see six women standing around the kitchen. Olivia, Savannah, Teal, Aurora, Catalina, and Skye. Over these past few days I've gotten to know all of them pretty well and they all seem to have the same story of how they ended up in York with a few unique details.

They all have a dashing man they started seeing.

A charity event held by the Bay Foundation.

The gold invitation box.

After I speak to enough of them, I realize that I need to incorporate a gold invitation box into my own origin story to fit in and I wonder how many of them are lying about theirs.

"So, so, so," Olivia says, pouring herself a cup of coffee. "What the hell happened to you last night?"

Her tone isn't accusatory, but inquisitive. She looks genuinely excited to hear all the juicy details. I shrug.

"There's no need to hide. We saw what happened."

This takes me by surprise.

Saw?

I don't remember seeing anyone else's dates when they went on them.

"Yeah, Mirabelle came by and asked if we wanted to watch," Savannah explains. "Apparently, there's a television channel which is basically just CCTV."

"So...you saw..." I start to say, nodding.

I don't know exactly where to go with this.

How much did they see?

How much did they hear?

I mean, I always knew that people up there, the judges and whoever else, were watching. But the women, too?

"Yes, we saw you kissing!" Olivia says excitedly.

I nod.

I should've expected this much. I mean, a part of me did, but for some reason I'm still surprised.

"Why did you go to the beach with him?" Savannah asks.

The others gather around me, their eyes wide with glee. Despite the fact that we are competing against each other, there is a feeling that everyone is genuinely excited for each other.

"He asked me to," I say, nodding my head. "He wanted to have some alone time."

"So, what happened when you were there?" Teal asks.

She is a quiet girl with short dark hair, and alabaster skin. We haven't had the opportunity to speak much since Olivia and Savannah have dominated my attention, but I had a feeling that we would get along. She mentioned that she was studying to be a librarian, and that was all I needed to know.

"You didn't see me?"

"No, there's no feed out there," Olivia says. "I have a feeling that Easton knew this."

I shrug. "Well, you didn't really miss much. We just ran down the beach and found this cave not far from there."

I mention the cave on purpose.

In case, they did watch me, I don't want to be caught in a lie. The best lies are always the ones which are closest to the truth.

"Oh, really?" Teal asks quietly. Her eyebrows go up with curiosity. "So, what happened then?"

"He just asked me more about my life. I asked about his. Getting to know each other type of thing."

"Is that all?" Olivia asks.

I debate whether I should tell them the truth. They already know that we had kissed, so what's one more kiss?

"Well, actually...that's where he kissed me!"

The girls make a loud cooing sound.

Their eyes light up and they demand to know the details. Just saying that it was a kiss is not enough.

What kind of kiss?

What did his mouth feel like?

How forceful was he?

Did he press you against the wall?

Did he press you against his body?

These details are important and I provide each and every single one. But I do downplay it.

Somehow, telling them everything feels too raw. And wrong.

"You know, he didn't kiss anyone else but you," Savannah points out afterward. I shrug.

"Yeah, why is that?" Aurora asks.

I don't know much about her, either, except that she has this attitude.

It's like she's ready to fight the world at any turn. Her dark mocha hair is pulled back in a loose bun and her hazel eyes shoot rays of anger in my direction.

"I don't know," I say. "I guess we made a connection. I mean, isn't that the point of this?"

"Do you think you'll sleep with him?" Aurora asks.

"No, of course not," I say a bit too quickly.

"Looks like he wants to sleep with you."

I don't know what to say to that.

So, I just meet her eyes and stare back at her. Hard.

People like Aurora see weakness in those who give them even an inch of latitude. And if she thinks I'm weak, then she will try to bully me even more.

This isn't my definition of weakness. It is in fact the bully who is weak and scared and ruled by her ego. But if I don't want her to bother me, I need to stand up to her.

"I don't have any control over that," I say confidently and wait until she breaks eye contact first.

After a few moments, she finally caves.

Is this what it feels like? To be a chameleon? I try to be the person that someone wants me to be.

Not for any other reason except that I need to survive.

I can't fight Aurora and I don't want to, but I do need her to respect me.

I do need her to not go behind my back and try to convince the girls to go against me.

I hate this manipulative, conniving person that I'm becoming.

No, correction.

I hate this manipulative person that I *am*.

But what other choice do I have?

CHAPTER 23 - EVERLY

WHEN I'M STARTLED...

Back in my room, I sit at my desk and stare at nothing in particular. Mirabelle was kind enough to bring me some books to read to pass the time. I have a television as well, but it seems to cloud my thinking, more than giving me space to think.

I haven't read these books before, but I know I should. They're classics. You know, the type of books that you always think you're going to get to sometime, but you never do. I read the first two chapters of Jane Eyre and let it sit open on my lap as I pick up the pen and start to write.

Just as before, my thoughts seem to crystalize when I press the pen to paper. I don't even know where they are going to take me, but I write and write until my hands cramp up.

Easton's name comes up within a few sentences and I know that I'm going to have to dispose of everything that I've written as soon as I finish, but I don't care.

I don't need to keep these words for later.

Chefs and cake bakers don't.

They make these perfect dishes and elegant designs and what do they do with them afterward?

Consume them.

So, that's what I'll do.

My thoughts return to Easton.

Easton Bay.

Easton *fucking* Bay.

Why are you here?

Why are you in my life?

How dare you infuse this place with your humanity?

He told me something that he should've kept to himself. I didn't need to know that his father had his fiancée killed. *That's the last thing I wanted to know!*

As I write these words, my hand cramps up something awful and I take a momentary break after the exclamation point.

I shake my head, having an invisible conversation with Easton.

Why did you tell, you idiot?

Why did I have to know?

Now, if I'm ever interrogated about it, they'll have something to use against me.

By interrogation, I mean, the kind that they use with force.

Torture.

Shivers run down my spine at the thought of that.

I know that I won't be able to stand up to them. I'm not good at handling pain. Some people are. Some people can put up with anything.

But me? No.

Oh, how I wish you had never told me a thing, Easton Bay.

I say his name out loud right after I finish writing it. It sounds good rolling off my tongue.

"Easton Bay," I repeat over and over.

Somehow, the more I get to know him, the more mysterious he seems.

Of course, I know exactly why he told me about who ordered the killing of Alicia. He felt like he needed to prove himself; to share something with me that I could use against him.

As I put these words onto paper, my hand starts to shake.

Fear creeps into me.

What if someone were to walk in, right now? What if someone were to confiscate these sheets of paper from me?

At first, I try to keep the fear at bay. Nothing is going to happen. Just write, I tell myself. And I do. My thoughts drift from Easton to the girls. I'm torn between my desire to get to know them better and my feeling of general hopelessness as to what would be the point?

I got to know Paige.

I liked her.

She became my friend.

And now what?

They sent her away to God-knows where.

Now, I have to spend my nights tossing and turning and thinking about what is happening to her. Somewhere in the back of my mind, I hope against hope. Perhaps, they did just send her home. It's not like she saw anything here like I did.

But that seems highly unlikely.

So, what about the other girls? Is it worth getting to know them better while we're here? Or would that make saying goodbye that much harder?

I put the pen down and look out the window. Then I begin to write again.

Just because pain will come with goodbye, that doesn't mean that this moment now should be forsaken.

I stare at the words in my haphazard handwriting and read them over and over. They seem to spring out of nowhere.

That's right.

Of course, it's right.

Living in fear is no way to live.

Life is short.

It may be shorter in York, and it may be crueler and harder.

So why then, forsake something that could give it some hope? Some love?

Meeting and talking and laughing with Paige added so much to my life here.

Yes, I miss her. Yes, I worry about her and I want to find her and free her. But just because a goodbye will be difficult later, it doesn't mean that the good shouldn't be experienced now.

In a world that is so limited on the good, why would I close myself off from whatever good I could find?

A loud, thunderous knock startles me, making

me nearly jump out of my seat. A second later, the door swings open.

"Please come down for the elimination ceremony," Mirabelle says.

My heart jumps into my throat.

Now? I look down at the desk.

She had come in here so suddenly that I didn't have time to do the one thing that I needed to do; get rid of my writing.

I spin around in my chair and try to make it seem like the papers on my desk aren't important at all.

"Okay, I'll be down in a second," I say.

When she looks around the room, I push the loose pieces of paper under my *Jane Eyre* with my elbow.

My heart is thumping so loudly through my head that I can barely hear a thing, but my hands remain steady. Calm.

"You know the rules, Everly," Mirabelle says, exasperated. "You have to come down now. I'm not going to ask you again."

I get up from my chair and follow her out. I hold my breath, hoping that she won't look at the table behind me.

I want to usher her out, but I don't want to be too eager.

When we leave the room, I let out a small sigh of relief. I may have gotten away with it now, but the papers are still there.

I need to get through this elimination fast so that I can get back and destroy the evidence.

CHAPTER 24 - EVERLY

WHEN I MAKE A CONNECTION...

*a*s I stand in line between Teal and Savannah, my thoughts keep circling back to my writing upstairs.

How could I be so stupid?

How could I write those things about Easton?

He trusted me in absolute confidence and I just wrote it down for everyone to see.

What an idiot!

"I'm glad I'm not the only one who didn't get the memo about the dress code," Teal jokes.

It takes me a moment to realize what she's talking about.

I look down and realize that I'm dressed in my pajamas. Not even yoga pants, which have basically become appropriate attire for everything from a conference to a lunch date.

But actual pajama pants!

Soft. Light. Loose. White with little pink flowers.

The top is a large, completely mismatching t-shirt. My hair is tied up in a bun, unwashed and covered with a thick layer of dry shampoo, which I doubt was fooling anyone.

I touch my forehead. Oily.

Whatever makeup I was wearing earlier that day, has all pretty much rubbed off.

"Perfect," I mumble to myself. "Just perfect."

"Don't worry about it," Savannah says. "You look fine."

I glance over at her.

Just like the rest of the girls except for Teal, she is dressed in a tight, black cocktail dress. Her hair is expertly blown out and her makeup looks as if it was airbrushed.

"Yeah, right," I say with a shrug.

"How is it that they all found out about this before we did?" I ask Teal.

She shakes her head.

I try to remember what we were all doing this morning after breakfast.

Oh, yes, of course.

We were hanging out at the pool. Tanning. Swimming. Gossiping. Drinking. But after a couple of drinks, I got a headache so I escaped to my room for a little rest and relaxation.

"I left the pool about the same time you did," Teal says.

Dressed in a pair of yoga pants and a tight-fitting white tank top, she doesn't look anywhere near the mess that I do.

"You look nice," I say.

She waves her hand and laughs, not believing me.

"They have a really nice library here," Teal says. "Do you like to read?"

My eyes open wide.

"Yes, I do!" I nod my head.

She gives me a wide, toothy smile. The last thing I would expect to talk about while waiting for the elimination round to begin is books, but it seems just as good a time as any. The consequences of what's to come are life-changing, so why not pass the time not thinking about them?

I bring up how I just started reading *Jane Eyre* and Teal tells me that it's one of her favorites.

"I never read it when I was younger. I mean, I

picked it up a few times, but the beginning was always kind of a turn-off."

"Yeah, it can be a bit difficult to get into. But it's beautiful. A gorgeous romance. Dark, brooding. Also, it has so much about Jane Eyre's interior life. That kind of writing was quite advanced for the time."

"Being a woman writer is advanced enough. And then showing that you have thoughts and feelings. I mean, god-forbid, right!" I say sarcastically.

"But don't get me wrong. Just because I love some classics doesn't mean that I don't appreciate what's going on in writing now. I mean, I spend practically all of my free time reading indie authors."

"Indie as in self-published?" I clarify.

She nods.

"Especially in romance. They are doing such advanced things. Authors in traditional publishing are just discovering dual narration. You know, when one chapter is written from one character's perspective and another is from another. But indie romance writers have been doing that for ages."

I smile and tell her how much I love reading those books, too.

"If you like books with plenty of thoughts and

feelings as well as some steamy scenes, those are definitely for you," she adds.

I love how Teal gushes about writing.

I have some online friends who love to read the same books I do - you know, what others might call a little smutty just because they have a sex scene or two or three - but it's rare to talk to someone in real life who shares this interest. And also someone who not only shares it, but also talks about it proudly.

"I actually want to pursue another master's degree," Teal says. "In popular fiction. They don't have many of them, but I would love to write a thesis about indie romance today. I mean, so many women I know read books like that. So many writers make a living, however meager, off their writing. And yet, there's very little scholarly discussion about these books."

We talk about the significance of the classics in the area, *Fifty Shades of Grey*, and how influential it was in encouraging other writers to step forward and start putting out their own fiction.

As we talk, our voices get louder and louder, until the other women start to give us disapproving looks.

But Teal just laughs.

For a girl who doesn't seem to exude much

confidence, it's amazing how nonchalant she is in dismissing them.

"The thing is that many people like to look down on that kind of literature," she whispers to me, laughing. "But who cares? They probably don't really like to read anyway since they read a book or two a year. Readers who like to read indie romance read. I mean, they really read."

I look at her, a little surprised. "What do you mean?"

"Well, I just have anecdotal evidence, but from what I found out, many read a few books a week, and some even a book a day."

I gasp at the number. "Really? Suddenly, I don't feel like much of a reader since I barely manage two or three books a month."

"I usually read like a book a week, but it's not a competition. It's just a matter of desire."

The more we talk, the more connected I feel to her.

Also, the more regretful I feel.

Why didn't I get to know her better sooner?

Why did I close myself off to this possibility of meeting this wonderful person who is so interesting to talk to?

"Have you ever thought about writing?" I ask.

Having given up on trying to penetrate our conversation, the other women have made their own circle a little bit away from us, and they are talking in hushed tones. I can't hear a word and I don't really care to either.

"Actually, I am. I mean, I have a few authors who I really like to read and one of them had this blog about how to write a romance novel. So, I thought, hmm, I have some ideas. So, why not give it a try?"

"Really?" I feel my eyes lighting up.

"Yeah. I mean, I didn't get too far. I don't have enough discipline but I'm going to keep trying if I'm not—"

Her voice drops off.

And suddenly, we both become keenly aware of our circumstances.

I don't know exactly how she got here, but by the look on her face, I know that her journey has not been an easy one.

CHAPTER 25 - EVERLY

WHEN THERE'S ANOTHER
ELIMINATION...

*I*t's hard to make plans when your life isn't your own.

It used to be a state of mind.

I used to think I had no choices, but then I came to York and realized just how constrained my choices could be.

A prisoner.

A captive.

And yet, what if this is another house of mirrors?

The idea comes out of nowhere as we stand waiting for the elimination.

The rules are theirs.

The party is theirs.

We do as they say.

Like children, right?

But like children, we can rebel.

We can stand up.

We can fight for what we want.

And like children, we will probably fail.

I don't know what standing up and fighting means quite yet, but for now the spark of the idea is enough.

I do know one thing, no matter what happens tonight, I will not go gently into that good night.

J comes out and gives us all a once-over. His lips actually make a little smile when his gaze meets mine.

Does he know something I don't?

Just like the rest of the contestants, I don't really know how the elimination is going to go.

I did make a connection with Easton, but will they use it against me?

Will it be my weakness?

My Achille's heel?

Whatever is decided has been decided already, so I try to make the best of it.

As my thoughts swirl around in my head, I try to push them out by turning to Teal and continuing our conversation.

"So, where did you grow up?" I ask her.

She looks as surprised by my question as the rest, but answers anyway.

The rest of the women give us dirty looks.

I ignore them and we continue to talk.

I tell her about myself as well.

We talk in somewhat hushed tones until J asks us to be quiet.

"Why?" I ask him.

"Pardon me?" He gasps at my insubordination.

"Nothing is happening yet," I say with a shrug. "It hardly seems to matter."

"This is a very important event, Everly," he says. "Very tense."

"Yes, it is," I agree. "A bit too tense actually. So, I thought why not make it a little bit easier on everyone?"

He doesn't really have an answer for me so I turn back to Teal who giggles and tells me about her family.

The rest of the women follow my cue and start to engage in their own conversations.

And the ripple of change begins.

It's not much, of course.

Just a few words exchanged in hushed tones.

But I feel proud.

What was previously an affair governed entirely by them and their rules is now slightly altered.

We do have power.

We do have the ability to impact change. They can't get rid of all of us.

The door opens and Easton walks through.

His face is grave and expressionless.

A thought rushes through my mind.

They may not be able to get rid of all of us, but they could get rid of the trouble maker; me.

Doesn't matter, Everly. That doesn't matter. Chances are you don't have much to lose anyway.

Just as before, Easton positions himself next to the podium and says a few words. They are forced, rehearsed, and required. This isn't him talking. We all nod and wait.

Familiar velvet boxes make their appearance. They are stacked one on top of each other and there are only six of them now. Not enough for all of us.

No matter how much I tried to push the reality of the situation away, it suddenly dawns on me. I will not see some of these women again.

Easton calls the first name.

Savannah.

I give her a warm smile and watch as she goes up

there and gets her velvet box. I wonder how much decision making power Easton has over all of this.

Other names are called.

One after another.

Suddenly, there are only a few boxes left.

As they start to dwindle down, I exchange looks with Teal.

She gives me a re-assuring shrug and I give her one back.

"It's going to be okay," she whispers.

I nod.

I'm pretty sure that we both know that we're lying, but sometimes a well-placed lie can make all the difference.

Two boxes left.

I close my eyes and plead for my name to be next.

I've given up trying to read Easton's face. It's as if there's a thick impenetrable plexiglass separating us from one another.

"Teal, please come up here," he says quietly.

I'm torn.

My heart is bursting with happiness for her.

She made it.

She won't be eliminated for now.

Yet, my heart is breaking, too.

For me.

There's one box left.

I have to come to the conclusion that I do not want to reach.

If he hadn't called my name yet, he probably won't at all.

It's probably all over for me. I don't stand a chance.

Teal glances over at me with a tear running down her cheek.

Now, I know what fate awaits me. I inhale deeply and gather my strength.

"Congratulations," I say with a smile.

She deserves to be happy.

After she picks up her velvet box, she takes her place in line next to me. I reach over and give her a warm hug. It feels good to wrap my arms around someone.

"I'm so, so sorry," Teal whispers into my ear.

"It's okay," I say.

"Please, please, we still have one more box," J interrupts.

Reluctantly, we pull away from each other and stand to attention.

Easton isn't meeting my eyes. He knows

something I will know soon. I've reached the end of the road.

This is it for me.

You can do this, I say to myself. Whatever is to come, you can survive it, just like you did here. You just have to believe it.

"I had a great time with all of you," Easton says slowly.

His voice is breaking a little.

There's sadness, tenderness, and regret in it.

The other girls look as petrified as I feel, but I know the truth. Those words are meant for me. He has to eliminate me because he doesn't have any other choice.

"Everly."

I don't hear him at first. He repeats my name again. And again. I look up at him.

"What?" I ask.

"Everly, will you please come up here?" he asks, looking a little surprised.

I stare at him, dumbfounded. What is he talking about?

"Is this a joke?" I ask.

"Everly, please don't be disrespectful," J says. "Now, go up there and get your prize."

I shake my head.

The problem with convincing yourself of something is that it makes it almost impossible to believe that the opposite is true.

Luckily, my body takes over and I walk up to the podium. Easton gives me a warm smile and hands me a small velvet box, similar to the one that I got before.

"Can I open it?" I ask.

Easton laughs and nods.

"Yes, please open your boxes now," J quickly adds.

When I lift the lid, the clasp makes a loud clicking sound as it snaps back, revealing a beautiful tear drop ring inside.

It's delicate in design and looks almost like an engagement ring.

"It's...breathtaking," I whisper.

Tears start to roll down my cheeks, not because of the ring, but what it represents.

"Aha! I see we have a winner!" J says after scanning everyone's boxes. "Everly, I guess you're the lucky girl."

CHAPTER 26 - EVERLY

WHEN I FIND OUT WHAT IT MEANS...

*L*ucky girl? Why? I look down at my ring and then at the contents of the others' boxes. None of them have rings.

"What does this mean?" I ask Easton.

"It means you are the lucky girl to have even more time with Easton," J announces.

A smile spreads across my face without my consent. I look up at him. He is also smiling, but only slightly out of the corner of his lips.

The extent of our feelings is hard to decipher, but we try anyway. Neither of us are fully aware of what could happen if anyone were to find out the truth.

"How much time?" I ask.

"A night," J announces. "But what you two do

there is entirely up to you."

Not like you all won't be watching, I want to add. None of that matters though.

I'm going to have a night with Easton.

This ring means more time.

To kiss him.

To be with him.

To...escape from this place.

Could this be it?

Could this be our way out?

I put Easton's ring on my right ring finger and watch as it catches the light. The sparkle blinds me for a moment.

"This ring is..." I whisper, lost in its beauty.

"That ring is a three-carat diamond and the band is platinum," J says. Someone behind me claps and cheers.

"Please take good care of it."

I nod.

"It is yours to keep," J clarifies. I look up at him.

"Like for good?"

He nods.

"Wow," I mumble.

Walking back to my place next to Teal, I cradle my hand.

What is the worth of this ring?

And I don't just mean in terms of monetary value. I don't know much about diamonds, but Savannah and Olivia gather around me and estimate it to cost about fifty-thousand dollars based on its size, clarity, and workmanship.

"More if it's a brand name like Cartier or Tiffany's," Olivia points out.

But to me, this ring holds so much more value than that.

It's an opportunity to spend more time with Easton.

And a chance to maybe, finally make a break from this place.

Lost in all the commotion and excitement of what just happened is the flip side of the elimination: the women who didn't make it.

I see their fallen faces as they say goodbye.

They don't have much here, but whatever they do have has already been packed by the servants.

They are not allowed to go back to their rooms and we all have to say our goodbyes here.

"Fuck this!" someone yells and lunges at me.

A moment later, I'm on the floor and she's hitting me in the face and pulling my hair. It takes me a moment to realize that it's Skye, the one I talked to the least. She's pinning down my arms with her

knees and the weight of her body is making it
difficult to breathe.

I try to kick her or toss her off me somehow, but
no matter how much I thrash around, I can't.

Finally, someone pulls her off me.

"This game is rigged!" Skye yells at the top of her
lungs and spits in my face. "He knows her. He's going
to pick her. None of you matter anymore."

Someone pulls her out of the front door.
Everyone is shouting and talking around me, but I
can't make out anything they're saying. My head is
buzzing and throbbing from the impact. My eyes
can't seem to focus on anything.

"Here, let me help you get upstairs," Teal says
quietly, putting her arms around my waist.

I lean on Teal and together we walk slowly to
my room.

I sit down on my bed and bury my hands in
my knees.

Tears roll down my cheeks.

"Are you hurt?" Teal asks.

I shake my head no.

"I just need to be alone," I whisper. She does as
I ask.

I sit on the edge of the bed with tears streaming
down my face. I'm not crying because she hurt me.

I'm crying for her.

And for the others.

Mainly, I'm crying because the stress of this place is making it hard to do anything else.

Skye's right.

Easton and I do have a connection, but whether that will end up being something that will benefit me remains to be seen.

And then...yes, of course!

I run over to my desk. The papers holding Easton's darkest secret is lying untouched just where I buried them. Deep within the pages of *Jane Eyre*.

I grab the book and go to the bathroom. I turn on the faucet and dunk one sheet at a time into the sink. The pages quickly become waterlogged. When I rip them down the middle, they come apart like room-temperature butter. The ink starts to run, but it's not enough. I rip the pages into smaller and smaller pieces and shove them into my mouth.

I will not make a mistake like this again.

Just as I swallow the last piece, there's a loud knock on my door and Savannah and Olivia come in, followed by Teal, Aurora, and Catalina. The only ones who are left.

Their presence startles me and I jump back.

"Hey, didn't mean to scare you," Olivia says. "But what the hell was that?"

"What?" I ask, washing and drying my hands.

"You getting the night with Easton." Savannah laughs. "C'mon, you know it's because of that kiss."

"You're reading Jane Eyre in the bathroom?" Aurora asks.

"Just started it," I say, nodding. Teal gives me a knowing look.

As they gather in my room to further dissect and inspect what has just occurred at the elimination, I let out a sigh of relief.

If I had waited even a minute longer before destroying what I had written, then they would've probably caught me with it.

And then what?

CHAPTER 27 - EVERLY

WHEN WE GOSSIP...

"*H*ow are you feeling?" Teal asks.

"I'm fine, really," I say over and over until neither of us believes it.

My head is still swimming and thoughts are not coming in as clearly as before.

My heart is racing so fast that it's about all I can hear in my head.

"She really got you good," Olivia says, rubbing my shoulders.

I nod, hanging my head.

"The thing is that you can't really blame her, right?" Olivia asks the whole room.

Some just nod in agreement, while others look at her surprised.

"Well, you know, I don't want to take her side, but, Everly, the game does seem a bit rigged."

"What do you mean?" I ask.

"You and Easton. That kiss. What is that all about?"

"We just had a connection and that's it," I say with a shrug.

I wonder if there's a moment when a rabbit peacefully sitting in a meadow realizes that there's a pack of coyotes after her. There has to be. Is this my moment?

"Why are you even spending the night with Easton?" Savannah asks. "Aren't we competing for the King's hand in marriage?"

Oh, yes.

In all the commotion, I have somehow forgotten the obvious.

"Are you going to sleep with him?" Savannah asks.

"With whom?"

"Easton. I'm assuming if you win, you will sleep with the King."

The thought hadn't really occurred to me until this moment and suddenly I feel sick to my stomach.

Why did I go on a date with Easton? Why did he

choose me to spend the night with? I mean, yes, I know why.

He chose me because he wants me, but what about this? All of this? What is the point?

"Maybe, it's a test," Teal suggests. "Maybe you're not supposed to sleep with him. Maybe it will get you disqualified."

"Very likely," I say.

"Maybe you shouldn't spend the night with him," Teal says.

I shrug. At this point, I'm completely at a loss as to what I should or shouldn't do.

"Or what if that were a lie," Savannah says. "What if the real prize is Easton, and they just threw in the King to lead us in a different direction?"

"Those are all...possibilities," I mumble.

The women start to talk among themselves.

Savannah and Olivia are certain that the ultimate prize is still the King, if he is someone you would call the prize, I wouldn't.

But the others aren't so sure.

I want it to be Easton, too. More than anything.

But would the King just let me have the one person that I really want?

"So, what are you going to do?" Teal asks while others are deep into their heated debate.

"I don't know. I'm just going to meet with Easton and see how it goes," I say.

"I am really glad that you got the ring," she adds. "When he called my name, I got so worried for you. There was only one box left."

"I know, I did, too," I mumble, unable to meet her eyes, feeling very guilty over the whole situation.

"She's the biggest threat we have here, ladies," Aurora says, making a large lump form in the back of my throat.

She waits for me to respond, but I don't.

"Easton likes her. A lot. And that's a problem. I just want you all to be keenly aware of this fact."

"He's not even the one we are supposed to be after," I say. "I mean, this might be a very bad thing."

"I'm not so sure," Aurora declares. "He's the King's son. He has his ear. I'm sure that he has a lot of influence."

Don't be so sure, I want to say, but I don't.

There's no way to win this conversation.

There's no way to convince her of something so...nonsensical.

So, I don't even bother.

I wish they would all leave so I can get some sleep. But they continue to talk and argue, their voices getting louder and more deliberate with each minute.

It's the tendency of the human condition to believe that you will be the one who will be doing the convincing if you just talk over the others.

As everyone is fighting for their chance to talk, no one is really listening to anyone else.

A moment later, the door swings open and Mirabelle appears.

WHEN SHE TAKES ME TO HIM…

Mirabelle doesn't say much as she leads me down the hallway. I'm not sure where we are going, but I'm glad that I grabbed a sweatshirt before I left.

The air conditioning is suddenly overwhelming my senses.

I wrap my arms around my shoulders, keenly aware of the goose bumps. It's going to be fine, I say to myself silently. I don't know why but a grip of anxiety suddenly runs through me. My heartbeat races, throwing my body into even more of a cold sweat.

"C'mon, hurry up," Mirabelle says.

"Where are we going?"

She leads me outside and down a familiar pathway.

The humidity is warm and comforting and I finally start to relax. When I see him standing in the doorway, all the tingles disappear completely.

It's him.

Easton.

He's waiting for me.

I run straight into his arms.

Tilting my head back, he presses his lips onto mine.

Whatever anxiety I felt only a few moments ago vanishes completely.

I want him.

I need him.

I crave him.

"Have a good time," Mirabelle says, walking away.

I mumble something in return as he closes the door behind us, but I doubt either of us can figure out what it is.

Easton grabs me by my waist and lifts me up. As I slide down his body, he kisses me.

First, the top of my breasts.

Then my neck.

Behind my ears. My chin. And finally, my lips.

Once our tongues touch, everything outside stops existing.

There's only him.

There's only me.

There's only us.

Forever.

"I missed you," he whispers.

He pulls away from me for a moment and runs his tongue up my neck, to just below my ear.

I toss my head back and moan.

"Oh my God, what happened?" Easton asks.

I open my eyes and see him staring at my face.

"It's nothing," I say, turning my head away from him so that the cut near my temple isn't as visible.

But that doesn't satisfy him. It's the last thing I want to talk about right now.

I want him to take me into his arms and make me forget about all that shit, but he has to know.

So, I shrug and tell him what happened at the elimination.

As he listens, his fists clench up and a bit of white appears on his knuckles.

"It's fine," I say. "Really, it doesn't matter. She was just...angry."

"She shouldn't have done that."

"She felt hopeless," I explain.

"Don't defend her."

"You don't know what it's like, Easton. To be so... at the mercy of everyone here."

"Oh, I don't?" he asks.

The tone of his voice changes.

This was not the direction that I wanted this night to go.

"No, not really. You are the son of the King."

"What does that matter?"

"The things that happen in York behind closed doors..." I start to say, but I can't make myself continue.

I don't know if anyone's listening. We are probably not alone. And I don't know what the consequences will be for me if I do come out and say all of these things.

"I just understand why she was so angry. And I don't blame her."

Darting his eyes around the room, Easton is also keenly aware of the cameras.

"You don't know what I do or don't know about York," he says quietly. And slowly I nod.

There's so much more that he wants to say, but he's keeping his mouth shut just like me.

He puts his arm around my waist again, but the moment is over. It's like suddenly there's a canyon between us, filled with everything that we want to say to each other.

"I hate this," I whisper.

"What?"

"That we can't...talk."

"We can."

"I know," I say, nodding my head.

We are both lying, but what else is there to do?

"There is something we can do," Easton says, giving me another kiss.

"But what about—" I say, looking up.

"They can watch if they want to."

I shrug. This doesn't feel right.

"What's wrong? Don't you want to?" he asks.

"Yes, of course, I want to. But what about...the competition?"

He looks at me perplexed.

"I mean, isn't the point of this whole thing for your father to find a wife? Isn't that strange that we're going to...you know. If I am to be your stepmother?"

That word lands like a blow. He looks at me.

"I'm his proxy, Everly," he says.

I know what those words mean, but I don't know what he means.

I stare at him. And then...suddenly, something occurs to me.

What if my first instincts about this were right?

What if this isn't a competition to marry his father?

What if that's just a play, a game of pretend?

Just like everything else is in this fucking place.

"What's going on here?" I ask.

"Nothing."

"I can feel that something is...wrong. I mean, is this competition really about your father?"

His face tenses up.

"What aren't you telling me, Easton?" I demand to know.

"I don't know for sure," he says slowly, carefully mulling over each word.

I wish he would just spit it out already, but he refuses. He looks around a bit, and then takes a deep breath.

"You're not supposed to know this," he says.

"Know what?"

"I just found out myself."

I wait for him to continue.

"My father has decided to not take a wife this time," he says slowly. "He just told us."

I nod and wait for him to continue.

This sounds like good news to me, but by the look on his face, I'm not so sure.

Where is this going?

What's going on?

"He will be picking two women for us to marry," he says.

"Us?" I ask.

"Abbott and I."

Abbott.

There's that terrible name again.

I thought I could get away from him. I thought that maybe he was gone for good. But, of course not.

"Why...um...when..." Questions keep popping into my head without any accompanying answers.

"Everly, I don't know if this is true or not. I mean, he can change his mind at any moment. This whole thing is just one elaborate game to him. Nothing special. It's something he does for fun."

"And now he's going to find you a wife?" I ask.

He nods.

"And you're not happy about that?" I ask.

"I have plans, Everly. To leave this place. For good after this. And now...now, I don't know."

He walks back and forth, pacing like a caged tiger.

There are things we shouldn't say and there are things we cannot.

I shouldn't talk about this.

But we absolutely cannot talk about what he told me about Alicia.

And yet, there are things that need to be said.

Planned.

Explained.

WHEN WE ARE ALONE...

"Let's go for a swim," I suggest. "I want to be somewhere private."

"Then we should go down to the beach."

We walk down hand in hand.

There's not a soul around, but that doesn't mean they aren't watching.

"I have to tell you," I say when I think we are close enough to the water so that the waves can hush some of my words. "I'm kind of relieved that this isn't about your father anymore."

"You shouldn't be," Easton says, shaking his head.

"But why?"

"My father doing this, isn't a good sign. He's

becoming more and more erratic. He has always been cruel and unforgiving and if you think he would just let us get married, you'd be very, very wrong."

I know that I should think about that. I should worry about it.

And yet, the only place my mind goes is what he had just said.

Marry him.

The thought of marrying Easton gives me butterflies in my stomach.

"If you could marry me, would you?" I ask shyly.

He looks at me, furrowing his eyes.

Then he shakes his head.

My hopes drop.

I'm such an idiot. What am I even thinking? This is neither here nor there. I need to worry about getting out of this place, not about whether Easton wants to marry me.

"Of course not," I say quietly. "I'm so sorry. I shouldn't have brought it up."

"Everly," Easton says, turning my whole body to face him.

The moonlight illuminates him, giving his whole face a soft cool icy glaze.

"I would marry you tomorrow, if I could," he

says. The words just hang there in mid-air between us.

This is the last thing that I ever expected to hear and yet it's the only thing I need to hear.

"I love you, Everly. And I will love you forever."

The world back home isn't devoid of love, compassion, and hope. It's not cruel, dark, and painful like this one. And yet, it is in this world that I have Easton.

"I love you, too," I say and stand up on my tiptoes.

Our lips touch.

I haven't said those words in a long time. I haven't felt anything close to love since I've been here, and yet...nothing is more true.

I stand close to him, timid and unsure. Darkness wraps around us, making me feel safe and warm. He stands towering over me. He is tall, broad-shouldered, and strong. Suddenly, he seems so much bigger than he did before. So much more powerful. He takes me into his arms and I know that he will protect me.

Easton's breathing remains calm. Even. He kneels down and kisses me again. He digs his hands into my hair, pulling me closer to him. Our faces touch. The touch is gentle and sweet. Familiar. It's like we have known each other for years, centuries even. It's not so familiar that it's boring. I don't know what to expect, but it feels comfortable. I look up at him. I haven't felt this at ease since I've been here. No, that's wrong. I haven't felt this at ease ever. No man has ever made me feel so...loved.

I pull away again to make the moment last longer. I want to look at him. I want to make sure that he's real. But this time, the mood changes. It's sudden, but intense. And very surprising.

Easton grabs me by my shoulders. He looks straight into my eyes and says, "I'm going to take you."

Shivers run down my spine. I cough a little, trying to catch my breath.

I glance at his lips. "I need you," he says and licks them.

I reach up and brush my fingertip over his lips. Then I take his head in my hands and press my lips onto his. The kiss is slow and deliberate. We are feeling each other out. We are getting to know each other. There's a tenderness that he exudes and I welcome. This moment is fragile and uncertain and we are still feeling each other out. And yet, there's something else here. There's a kind of passion that I only thought existed in books. I yearn for him. I need to feel his touch. I have to have his hands on my body. I stand up on my tiptoes. I press my body into his. I wrap his arms around me. But it's not enough. Our clothes are in the way.

With every moment that our lips are locked onto each other's, there's a warmth that flows from the core of my body outward. Easton's breathing gets more rushed and I taste each breath that he expels. His hands make their way up and down my back, but after a few minutes, it's not enough. He pulls my shirt over my head. Looking down at me, his eyes grow wide and hungry. He craves me. He wants my body more than I ever saw anybody want anything.

Pressing his mouth against my neck, his kisses become more harried and hungry.

"I have to have you," he mumbles, moaning into my ear. He gives me a little nibble on the top of my shoulder. It's a playful bite. It's just for fun. It hurts a little, but only enough to make me want him even more.

After unclasping my bra, he lets the straps slide down my arms. It's warm and humid outside. The breeze is soft and inviting, but I start to shiver. Goose bumps run up and down my arms from the excitement of what is about to come, what he is about to do to me. He drops my bra onto the sand on top of my shirt and looks at me in the moonlight. My nipples stand up as if at attention. They harden just from his gaze, and they become sharp enough to cut through glass when he places one of them in his mouth.

Easton pulls on my hair, tilting my head back. My neck becomes exposed to his touch and he runs his fingers up and down my neck, toward my breasts. He keeps his lips on my breasts, giving each one equal attention. With the other hand, he cups my breast, massaging one and then the other. He gathers my hair in one big handful and gives me a strong tug with each kiss. After a few moments, it becomes too much and I try to straighten back out.

"Stay," he says.

His command makes me lose my footing for a moment. But he steadies me, by grabbing my waist.

"Stay put," he says, planting me firmly into the ground. I lick my lips. I haven't seen this version of Easton before and it makes my nipples even harder. I love how he takes control of my body, allowing me to relinquish myself to him.

CHAPTER 30 - EVERLY

WHEN THERE'S MORE...

*A*s I stand before him, he gets down on his knees. My breasts are right at his mouth level and he trades his lips for his hands. I don't know which I enjoy more. His hands are strong and powerful, but when they cradle my breasts, they are soft. His fingertips are almost effervescent. His lips and tongue, on the other hand, are flirtatious and mesmerizing. I have never been so...adored before.

As he stands before me, my hands find their way to his hair, burying my fingers deep within the thick strands. I drop one hand into the crook of his arm. The muscles underneath my fingertips curl and flex with each move. His skin is soft to the touch, but it is the strength in his taught muscles that sends waves of warmth through my core.

He comes back up to my mouth, giving me one last kiss. Then he breathes hard into it and pulls off his shirt.

When he looks down at me, his eyes are big and wide. They look at me with adoration as if I'm the most beautiful woman in the world.

He kisses me behind my ear again, nibbling on my earlobe. He breathes in and out and I hear the echo deep inside.

He wants me.

It's as if he is desperate for me.

It sounds almost like a growl.

Easton moves his hands to my hips and pulls off my pants. It takes one strong yank and they come off. Then he kneels down before me and slowly pulls down my underwear.

He nibbles at the lace near my hipbones and follows them with his mouth as he pulls them off my hips. I place my hands on top of his shoulders and run them up and down his neck.

His shoulders are wide and powerful, each muscle expands and contracts with each breath. When he removes my underwear, I hold on to him for balance.

Suddenly, I'm naked. No, not naked, but nude. I'm not exposed.

I am loved.

He looks at my body with adoration.

I have a lot of insecurity with my imperfections, yet he doesn't see any of them. I look at him in return.

Each muscle in his stomach flexes and relaxes. His body is chiseled, taut and tan, the kind of body I've only seen in the movies. He looks as if he were airbrushed.

"You are beautiful," he says and I blush.

"Your body is...amazing," I mumble as he kisses me again.

When he pulls away from me, he gets down on his knees and opens up my legs. He kisses my thighs and then deeper inside of me. He opens me up as his fingers find their way in. My legs start to feel weak. Warmth starts to spread through my body.

"I have to sit down," I say.

"Wait."

I watch as he gathers our clothes and then carefully helps me down onto them. The romance of making love on the beach can be quickly squashed by the reality of sand getting into everywhere.

As I lie down on the blanket of clothes, Easton lowers himself on top of me. His hard and thick cock presses hard into my pelvic region. I reach down for it to feel it with my hand.

It's large and smooth and thick. My legs open wide for him and he slides inside.

Now, we are one.

As he thrusts in and out of me, nothing else matters.

The sand feels cool and soft under my back and it accommodates our movements. With Easton inside of me, nothing and no one can hurt me.

It's as if our bodies were made for each other.

Warmth starts to build in my core.

I tilt my head back and give out a long moan.

He says my name over and over again as his movements start to accelerate. With each thrust, he goes deeper and deeper inside me.

When he gets close, he moans right into my ear, "Oh...Everly!"

"Stay with me," I mumble as I feel myself getting close.

He continues to hold onto me tightly, pushing deeper inside of me.

And that's when it happens.

An explosion.

Ripples of pleasure spread throughout my body.

My legs go numb.

Even my vision gets a little blurry.

"Easton," I yell into his ear digging my fingers into his back.

"I love you, Everly," he says kissing me over and over again.

PART 4

CHAPTER 31 - EASTON

BEFORE...

*R*ight before the elimination, my father calls me into his office. I've come to dread this, but I gather my strength and go inside. There's no use fighting it.

Just as before, I find him sitting at his large desk, reading a book. He doesn't look up at me until he turns the page and finishes the chapter.

I wait.

This is his game and I let him play it.

"Thank you for coming, Easton," he finally says, closing the book.

I glance at the cover. It's Harper Lee's *To Kill a Mockingbird*. I've given up trying to figure out what a man like my father could get out of a book like that.

"What do you think about Everly?" He comes right out and asks.

I look at him, trying to gauge what my answer should be.

After a moment, I give him a small shrug.

"You like her, don't you?"

"I don't really have an opinion about her," I finally say.

"Now, c'mon, that's not what it looks like to me."

I inhale deeply.

"I don't care either way," I say after a moment. "I mean, she's just a girl."

My father furrows his brows and then gives me a coy smile out of the corner of his mouth.

"I know that we don't always see eye to eye, son, but my intentions are not bad in asking you this."

I glare at him, completely unconvinced.

"You don't trust me?" he asks innocently.

"No, I don't like her," I finally say. "She might end up being my stepmother."

"We both know that's a lie," my father says, getting up from behind his desk.

He walks around the room slowly.

"Since I know that you like her, I thought of maybe changing up a few things about this competition."

My heart starts to beat faster, but I don't make a move or a sound. I wait for him to continue.

"I was wondering what you would think about possibly choosing a wife for yourself?"

The words take me by surprise. I have never considered this as a possibility.

"Is this a joke?" I ask.

"No."

"Why...? Why would you want to do that?" I ask.

"You and Abbott are getting on in years. It's about time I had some grandchildren."

I shake my head, more from shock rather than disagreement.

My father's loud laugh thunders around the room and leads him into a long speech about the importance of family.

"You see, despite how many new children I have, I have always been and will always be partial to you and Abbott. You are your mother's children, after all. My first wife's."

THE MENTION of my mother ticks at my heart, but I clench my jaw and continue to bear his words.

"When you get older, you will understand the meaning of family a lot more. It represents so much more than just the individual family members. It becomes your legacy."

No, your legacy will be the atrocities that happen on this island, I want to say. Your legacy is the hate and suffering that you foster.

My father drapes his arm around my shoulder and gives me a kiss on the cheek.

"None of us are getting any younger, my son. I want to play with some grandchildren before I get too old."

Even if they are the same age as your children? I want to ask, but again I bite my tongue.

"Don't you have anything to say?"

"I'm not sure what you want me to say."

"Do you want any of the women here?"

The question comes with so much gravity that it nearly crushes me under its weight.

"I thought I would offer you first pick of the litter so to speak, before I asked Abbott."

I nod, taking it all in.

"Yes," I finally say. "Yes, I like Everly very much."

"Good, that's settled then," my father says. I wait for him to elaborate.

"What is?" I ask after a moment.

"Oh, Easton, don't be so dim-witted."

I stare at him. It's not that I don't understand

what he's saying. It's just that the words don't really make any sense. Is he really talking about letting me marry Everly?

"Do I have to spell it out for you?" He asks.

I nod.

"Tonight, at the elimination you will chose the one you want to marry and give her a ring."

A smile forms at the corners of my lips.

"If you want my advice, you should take her for a ride in the sack before you make your final decision. The last thing you want is some frigid cunt."

His misogyny and disrespect makes me want to punch him, but I don't say a word. He has just given me everything I wanted.

He continues to talk about not only the importance of marrying well, but also for marrying someone you have affection for.

He doesn't mention the word love, just *affection*.

Apparently, he has made this mistake a few times.

"You also don't want to marry anyone stupid. They will make you look bad no matter what you do," he says.

I wonder where my mother fits in all of this, but he doesn't mention her.

I stand before him and listen until the speech is

over, and all throughout my thoughts keep circling back to Everly.

My future wife.

That is, if she will have me.

A loud knock on the door interrupts him, and Abbott walks in. He has sunken eyes and sallow skin, as if he hasn't slept in days.

His t-shirt is dirty and ripped at the collar and his hair is wild and oily.

"Why do you look like that?" My father gasps. "You look terrible."

"You sent me to Hamilton, remember," Abbott says with an accusatory tone, rubbing his unshaven face. "I came straight from there."

"Oh yes, of course," Father waves his hand in the air. "I forgot."

"If you had ever stepped foot in there, you wouldn't ever forget that place," Abbott whispers under his breath.

My father doesn't hear him.

Instead, he continues his speech about the importance of a good marriage. We listen, occasionally exchanging looks. Father drones on and on, finally coming to his point.

"Abbott, you need a wife. The contestants have

been narrowed down sufficiently, leaving only the creme de la creme. I'd like you to pick your wife from the ones who are left."

"I'll take Everly," Abbott says without missing a beat.

CHAPTER 32 - EASTON

WHEN HE SAYS HER NAME...

*A*bbott looks at me when he says her name.

Is this a challenge? He gives me a small knowing smile. I clench my jaw and ball up my fists.

"Everly? Huh?" Father laughs. "What is it with this girl? Maybe I should spend a little more time with her."

My blood is starting to boil. A familiar knot forms in the pit of my stomach. It throbs as if a bile of anger is oozing out of it.

"You don't know anything about Everly," I say in a cool, calm tone.

I inhale deeply trying to calm myself down.

Don't take the bait, I say to myself.

Don't let them see you sweat.

"I know that you don't want me to have her," Abbott says.

"That's not a good reason to take a wife, son," Father says shaking his head.

"She landed me in Hamilton," Abbott says under his breath.

This time, Father hears him. "Actually, you landed yourself there. You and your temper."

Abbot stares daggers at me.

"Okay, let's make this fair, then. Easton, you have been on a date with all the contestants already. So, why don't you, Abbott, do the same? Take them out, talk to them, see what you think."

"Even Everly?" I ask, trying to hide my shock.

"Yes, even Everly," Father says decidedly.

* * *

I FOLLOW Abbott out of our father's chambers ready to fight. My fists are balled up so much that the whites of my knuckles are showing.

My steps are hard and deliberate.

My back is tense.

Every part of my body is ready to throw and take a punch.

But Abbott surprises me. He turns around and wraps his arms around me in a warm embrace.

"What are you doing?" I ask.

"I missed you," he says.

I try to push him away, but he just pulls me closer.

"I'm sorry," he finally says, rubbing the mist in his eyes.

Is that a tear?

I did not know that Abbott Bay was capable of anything close to that.

"I'm sorry," he says again. "I'm just really tired. I haven't slept in…a long time."

"What happened in Hamilton?" I ask quietly, feeling the muscles in my body starting to relax.

"Um…nothing. Nothing special," Abbott says, turning away from me.

"I don't believe you."

He shrugs.

Whatever happened in Hamilton must've been something horrible. I have never seen my brother act this way before.

He has always been a loud, pompous prick.

And this tenderness?

This humanity that he's exhibiting now?

This isn't like him.

"You can tell me, you know," I say.

I'm putting myself out on a limb. Maybe it's a mistake.

"I don't want to fucking talk about it," he snaps and walks away from me.

I don't follow him.

Instead, I go down another hallway, taking the long way down to my place.

"Everly!" Abbott yells on top just as I'm about out of earshot.

"What?" I yell back.

He's standing far in the distance.

All I can see is his silhouette, but the way the acoustics work, his voice comes in loud and clear.

"Everly!" He says, with a loud, evil laugh. "She's mine!"

* * *

I WALK outside shaking my head. This time I'm angry with myself. Just as I thought that there may be an inkling of something human in him, he vanquished it completely.

Abbott Bay is exactly the person I always knew he was.

Some of my first memories are of him sitting on

top of me with a pillow over my head. He was trying to suffocate me and make it look like an accident.

When our mother caught him, he lied and pretended that we were just playing a game. When she asked me if that were true, I said yes because I was so afraid of him.

Abbott Bay is evil.

Whatever inkling of emotion I just saw back there that was just a pity party thrown in his own honor.

He may have suffered in Hamilton, I have no doubt about the fact that he did. But instead of focusing that anger on our father, the person who sentenced him to that place, he will take out his anger and frustration on Everly or anyone else he deems to be weaker than him.

He is a coward and a first-rate bully.

I have to do everything in my power to protect her from him, but what?

My mind races a mile a minute in search of an answer. But nothing occurs to me.

If I attack him now, Father will likely throw me into Hamilton as well. Then, I will be even further away from her.

No, I need to create some sort of diversion.

I need to buy time.

He has to be stopped.

From doing what exactly?

I know that he is capable of a lot of darkness, but will he do that on a date?

While everyone is watching? No.

He reserves his dark deeds for private moments.

Perhaps, going on a date with him is one of the safest ways that Everly could be with him. In public.

But then again, I managed to have alone time with her. I'm sure he could, too.

I don't know what to do. I don't have a solution.

Just a myriad of possibilities and outcomes that all lead nowhere good.

There is one thing I can do. I can warn her.

My walk turns into a trot and then an outright run.

I pick up my feet and race back to the main house. I run upstairs to her room and burst through the door without knocking.

It's empty.

I try the other girls' rooms.

They are empty, too.

Where did everyone go?

CHAPTER 33 - EVERLY

WHEN I CAN'T ESCAPE…

My heart is beating. I'm sitting in a large recliner with my feet up. There's a box of Milk Duds on my lap and one melting in my mouth. The room is dark and Teal's face is bathed in a soft blue light coming from the screen in front of us.

I wish we were watching a movie, but we aren't.

We are watching their date; Abbott and Catalina.

She's the first one to go.

I'm next.

Teal is holding my hand, whispering that it will be okay.

All I can think about is all the ways that it will not.

Abbott is acting polite and cordial. Catalina

looks beautiful and like she's having a good time.
Is she?

Abbott and Catalina don't know each other, but
he knows me. I don't know what's going to happen
on my date with him except that I doubt that it will
go as smoothly.

I can't bear to watch their dinner any longer.

The long pauses.

The smiles.

The conversation about nothing in particular.

The room feels like it's closing in around me. I
jump out of my chair and run outside.

I try to gather my breath, but it seems to
escape me.

When I was eleven, I tried to do a spin in the air
off the monkey bars after watching the girls'
gymnastics team at the Olympics on television. I was
so inspired that I just decided to go for it. I flipped
up in the air, did half a turn and landed flat on
my back.

Everything turned to black.

I couldn't feel any part of my body at first except
for my chest, which wouldn't let me take a full
breath of air.

Standing in this hallway, I feel the same way. It's
as if the wind got knocked out of me.

My thoughts drift back to Easton and the night that we had spent together. The closeness and safety that I felt just a little bit ago is gone.

Lying in his arms, I thought that everything was going to be okay.

But what about now?

Abbott is back and my dream of a happily ever after is shattered.

What if I make a run for it?

I could take off right now. I could just go, but where?

To escape from an island, I need things.

I need a plan.

I could hide out in the cave that Easton took me to, but for how long? I would need supplies there as well.

I don't know anything about this island.

I don't know how to drive a boat.

I don't know where I should even go if I had a boat.

No, to escape this place, I need help.

No, if I'm going to make a run from this place, everything has to be thought out. And hopefully, Easton would be part of it as well.

"Are you okay?" Teal asks, coming out of the theater room.

I nod.

My heart beat has slowed down and my breaths are calm.

"It's going to be okay, Everly," she says.

"Yeah, I know," I say with a nod. "I just got a bit freaked out."

"He's not going to do anything to hurt you. I mean, it's all televised. Everyone is watching."

I take a deep breath. She's right.

One of the things that I hated the most about the place, the surveillance, is now going to be the one thing to keep me safe.

"Yeah, you're right," I say. "It's all going to be fine."

Mirabelle comes out into the hallway.

When Teal tells her that I'm just a little rattled by the whole idea of going on a date with Abbott, she says that it can't be helped.

"The King is making some changes to the competition. I'm not exactly sure what's going to happen. This date isn't exactly a planned event."

Changes to the competition?

Easton told me about this, but he didn't mention Abbott.

Why does it have to involve going on a date with *him*?

"I'll be right back," I say and start to walk away.

"Where are you going?" Teal asks.

"I have to find Easton."

"You can't," Mirabelle says.

I stop dead in my tracks. What? Why?

"But my date with him isn't for a while, right?" I ask politely.

My head starts to pound so loudly that I can barely think. All I can hear is blood rushing through my arteries.

"You're next," Mirabelle says.

I stare at her, dumbfounded. I hear the words that she is saying, but they don't make any sense.

A door slams shut and Catalina emerges. She has a big smile on her face and a glow around her whole body.

"What are you doing here?" Teal asks.

"It's your turn," Catalina whispers and glides past us as if on a cloud.

"I don't understand," I turn to Mirabelle.

"These aren't long dates like you had with Easton. They're just meet and greets."

I stand staring at her.

She takes me by my shoulders and turns me toward the doors leading to the dining room where he is waiting for me. With a strong nudge, she pushes me through them.

Whenever there's anything you dread, it will inevitably come sooner than you think it will. My date with Abbott comes within a blink of an eye.

As Mirabelle pushes me toward the double doors, I raise my hands up to block them from hitting me in the face.

I hold my breath.

I don't want this to happen.

But it's too late to turn around.

It's too late to run.

It's going to be okay, I say to myself. Everyone is watching.

He's not going to do anything to hurt you. Not yet, anyway.

When I open my eyes, I see Abbott. Dressed in a casual t-shirt and jeans, he is eagerly waiting on the other side.

"Welcome! Welcome!" He says in an uncharacteristically exuberant manner. "I've been expecting you!"

CHAPTER 34 - EVERLY

WHEN I GO ON A DATE...

*T*ake a deep breath and step into the dining room. Abbott leans on the wall and looks me up and down. He is nowhere near me, but his gaze feels as strong as his touch. As he runs his eyes over my body, I feel myself cowering away from him. My body contorts and bends to create a protective cocoon around itself.

No, I say to myself, and straighten out my back, largely against my will. I stand up tall and raise my chin even higher.

"Come, sit, sit," he says, showing me to the dining room table.

I take a seat across from him without saying a word.

It's time to make a decision.

How will I react to him?

Should I go along and pretend like nothing has happened?

Should I play a role?

Should I confront him?

Fight him with words?

Abbott looks me up and down again. His gaze focuses on my breasts. I clench my jaw. When he licks his lips, it takes all of my will power not to grab the glass next to me and smash it over his head.

I'm not a violent person at all. I've never been in a fight. Yet, there's something about Abbott that makes it difficult for to me keep myself contained.

"Aren't you going to ask me how I am?" Abbott asks.

A question.

I didn't expect that.

I shrug and look away.

I don't cast my eyes away in fear, however. Instead, I look away as if I don't care.

"Well, let me tell you anyway," he says, leaning back in his chair.

I wonder if he has been practicing this.

"Hamilton was no joke."

I don't know what he's talking about, so he elaborates.

"My father sent me there after our little...interaction."

Nice choice of words, I want to say. But I keep my mouth shut and just listen. Not because he intimidates me, but because I don't want to speak to him. Ever.

"Anyway, it was some sort of punishment, you know how my father is. Always trying to teach lessons. Even to adults."

Just because you're an adult in years doesn't mean you're an adult in maturity, I say to myself. I'm sure you could stand to learn a lesson or two.

"But anyway, this isn't a sappy story about all that time I had to do hard labor, don't worry," Abbott says. "This is about something else."

There's a glint in his eyes. I wait for him to continue.

But he doesn't. I don't say anything.

If he wants to have this conversation with me, he can have it all on his own. It's not that I'm not curious.

It's a power thing. Not speaking to him is the only power I have at this moment, and I'm going to exercise it. It's my resistance.

After a few moments, he takes the bait. The

expression on his face tells me that he can't hold back. The news is just too good.

"I saw Jamie," Abbott finally says. "Remember Jamie? Oh yeah, I can tell that you do!"

There's a pause.

I don't know what to say, so I just wait.

The silence is killing me, but the alternative is even more scary.

But why is he there?

"Yeah, apparently, my father, in all of his wisdom, decided to send him there. Or maybe it was the decision of one of his many advisors," Abbott says, as if he's able to read my mind.

"He and I had a little chat about you. Apparently, you made quite an impression."

My lips grow chapped, but I don't dare lick them. I just sit there. Motionless. Not so much unwilling to move, but more like unable to.

"Do you have nothing to say?" Abbott suddenly roars at me.

There it is.

There's the other version of him.

The scary version.

The impatient, weary, frightening one.

I lift up my head and meet his eyes.

I keep my lips closed.

Pursed.

"So, what are you just not going to talk to me now?" he asks.

I don't respond.

"Oh I see, you don't think I have enough of a reason to be mad at you. You want me to be even angrier?"

I don't want anything, but for you to leave me alone. Just leave me alone.

I should say this out loud, yet I remain silent.

Abbott jumps out of his seat.

In a few steps, he's right next to me. I can feel his breath on my neck. I turn my nose from his minty fresh smell. He had just swished his mouth with mouthwash, but it's not enough to cut through his stench of cigarettes and liquor.

He's leaning over me.

His face is nearly touching mine.

I remain motionless.

On the outside, I'm unfazed.

Calm.

Collected.

On the inside, I'm trembling.

"Jamie said he really wanted to fuck you," Abbott whispers into my ear. "He said that's one of his biggest regrets about being here. That he didn't get the chance to fuck you. Hard."

Shivers run down my spine, but the expression on my face doesn't change.

"I promised him something," he continues. "I promised him that I would do it for both of us."

Whether it's a threat or a promise, I'm not sure. But it's enough.

I turn my head toward him and say, "Fuck you."

"That's the spirit!" Abbott exclaims at the top of his lungs and steps away from me.

I look down at my hand. Balled up into a fist, it's ready for combat.

I've never punched someone before, but whenever I come in contact with him, it's like my body gets ready before my mind does.

"I knew I could get some words out of you, Everly," Abbott paces in front of me with an exuberant look on his face.

CHAPTER 35 - EVERLY

WHEN HE PLAYS A GAME...

J'm angry with myself for letting him get the best of me.

"So, what do you think?" Abbott asks. "Do you think we'll have a good time?"

I stare at him and again say nothing.

He got one rise out of me, and that's enough.

I cannot control what he says, but I can control how I respond.

He can't make me do anything I don't want to do.

Not now, anyway.

"Okay, okay," Abbott says in his mocking voice. "Don't look at me like that. I know you have your hopes up, but you and I both know that we can't exactly do anything like that right now."

I shake my head.

Does he really think I'm sorry about that?

Is he that delusional?

No, he's just mocking me.

"Hey, do you know the story of the whipping boy?" Abbott says.

His eyes light up in glee. I don't respond, but I wonder where he's going with this.

"Well, back in the day, whenever a prince or some high ranking member of the royal family did something wrong, he'd have to get whipped. That was the way you learned your lessons back then. But the problem was that the teacher or the adult who was to bestow the punishment on him was a lower rank than the kid. So, what did they do? Well, they would bring in this other kid, the whipping boy, who would take the punishment for him."

The expression on my face doesn't change, but my whole body is thrown into a cold sweat.

I had no idea that anything like this existed, but just the thought of an innocent boy taking someone else's punishment makes my heart break.

"So, where am I going with this?" Abbott asks. "Well, that's the thing. Just because I can't have fun with *you* right now, doesn't mean that I can't show what I'm going to do you *later*."

My heart jumps into my throat and I can't

breathe. My hands turn to ice and my whole body begins to shake.

"Don't worry, don't worry. It's not going to hurt, *yet*," Abbott says and laughs out loud. His laugh is loud and thunderous, echoing around the dining room.

The side door suddenly swings open and a girl I don't recognize is brought in. She looks terrified. She is dressed in nothing but a tank top and a pair of white underwear. Her bare feet dragging on the parquet floor, makes her look even more naked and vulnerable. Two guards hold her by each arm so that she can't get away.

"What are you doing?" I jump out of my seat.

"Oh, there you go! I knew I could get something out of you."

I walk over to the girl to try to help her, but the guards pull her away.

Abbott jumps over to us and gets in between me and the girl.

"Get out of my way," I say.

"Fine," he says, taking a step back.

He raises his hands up to his shoulders so I can see his palms.

He's pretending to give up and surrender.

"What are you going to do now?" he challenges

me.

I'm not entirely sure.

It takes me a moment to find my voice, but when I do, I walk right over to the guards and tell them to let her go. They do by dropping her, face first, to the floor.

"Are you okay?" I whisper, kneeling down next to her.

She starts to say something in another language, one that I do not recognize.

"C'mon, let's go," I say, helping her up and allowing her to lean on me.

I lead her out of the dining room, toward the other exit. But before we get to the door, Abbott intercedes.

"You see," he says, putting his arm on my shoulder. "This isn't how the story of the whipping boy, or in this case, the whipping girl, goes."

I clench my jaw and try to walk around him.

This time, instead of simply blocking me, he grab's the girl's arm and pulls her away. Tired and spent, she falls to the floor.

"Now, go over there and sit," he says. "And watch."

I shake my head no.

"You do what I say, bitch," he says, pushing me to

the ground.

I get up, dust myself off, and stand before him.

Again, I shake my head.

This time, he grabs me by my arms and physically drags me over to the chair. He sits me down, by pressing really hard on my shoulders.

I wince in pain and try to get up again.

He raises his hand to me and slaps me right across the face. My cheek burns, as if something boiling hot was sprayed against it.

"You sit still and watch, or next time that will be a punch," he threatens.

Somewhere out of the corner of my eyes, I see him wave to the guards.

My vision is still blurry from how hard he has slapped me, so I don't see them well until they are right next to me.

I try to move, but I can't.

Their hands are firmly planted on my shoulders, keeping me in place.

Then the girl begins to scream.

Her voice is so loud and piercing that it sends shivers down my whole body.

The spots in my vision start to disappear and I shut my eyes to not see what he's doing to her.

Her screams turn into pleads of mercy.

I hear her trying to fight him.

I hear her begging for him to stop.

I hear him laughing.

But all throughout this, I keep my eyes shut.

I can't bear to watch.

I can't bear to see.

I tried to help her, but I failed.

She wouldn't be here if it weren't for me.

Tears stream down my face as this reality dawns on me.

How many other people are where they are because of me?

Every woman who was eliminated, whom I beat out, is now probably facing this same fate.

And yet, here I am.

Unscathed.

I drown out her screams with my thoughts.

I've become an expert at escape.

It takes me a few moments to remember just how to use my mind to get away from here, but then I just disappear.

The guards are no longer holding me.

The girl is no longer getting hurt.

I'm no longer in this room listening to the pain.

And best of all?

In this other world, Abbott doesn't exist at all.

CHAPTER 36 - EVERLY

WHEN IT ALL GOES TO BLACK...

Some people are capable of uncountable evil. If a person kills one person, he will get a life sentence.

If he kills a few he will get the death penalty.

If he kills more than ten, he will probably be sent away to a hospital and put into a padded room to be studied by doctors.

But if he kills a thousand? Or a hundred thousand or a million? What about those dictators who kill many millions? What becomes of them?

I don't know for sure if Abbott has killed anyone, but I wouldn't be surprised to learn that he has.

There's a darkness in him, the depths of which I haven't seen before.

He doesn't just go through the motions.

He enjoys this.

He enjoys inflicting pain and suffering.

After a while, the girl stops protesting. She stops fighting and she stops screaming. She just lets it happen.

But Abbott continues.

Does he think he won? I wonder.

I continue to keep my eyes closed. When her cries die down, it becomes easier for me to take my mind elsewhere.

"Oh c'mon, Everly!" He yells my name, breaking me out of my trance. "You have to watch. We're having so much fun here."

A sharp pain shoots up my spine as the guards' thick sausage fingers dig further into my shoulders. I winch as I turn my face further away from the scene.

And then...suddenly....Abbott stops.

The guards' let go of me.

When I hear the sound of shuffling feet and a pair of loud heels stomping toward me, I open my eyes.

Mirabelle is standing in the doorway, surrounded by five guards.

"What is going on here?" she asks.

Abbott lifts himself off the girl and pulls up his pants.

When he looks up at her again, his eyes are big like sand dollars.

Blood drains away from the surface of his skin as it turns a pale green color.

"What's going on here?" Mirabelle asks again.

And again, Abbott doesn't respond.

"This isn't...appropriate," she adds.

That's one word for it, I say to myself.

A more accurate description would be it's wrong, illegal, criminal.

"Everly and I were just having a bit of fun," Abbott finally says.

I'm about to say something in response, but Mirabelle focuses her eyes on mine and gives me a slight shake of the head. She's telling me to keep my mouth shut.

"As I'm sure you know, your date is being televised. All the other contestants, as well as the judges, and your Father are watching," Mirabelle says without acknowledging Abbott's previous statement.

"No, I didn't know," Abbott whispers under his breath.

"What was that?" Mirabelle asks.

"Does this look like the face of someone who knows?" he asks, raising his voice.

BACK IN MY ROOM, I sit in the recliner by the bed and wrap my arms around my knees. None of what he did there happened to me, but somehow it was worse.

Abbott is angry with me and he took it out on a total innocent.

My body starts to shake as the events of the evening come back to me in flashes.

I feel dirty just thinking about it.

I run to the bathroom and brush my teeth. Then I brush them again.

I swish a cap of mouthwash around my mouth until my tongue feels like it's on fire, but I can still taste and smell his scent on me. That disgusting mixture of liquor, mixed with cigarette smoke, mixed with hatred and anger.

Climbing under the covers, I begin to cry.

Easton, where are you?

Come to me.

I need you.

I send him mental messages hoping that somehow they can reach him.

* * *

I'M NOT sure how much time passes while I lay in bed. Catalina, Olivia, Teal and Savannah come into my room to comfort me, but nothing they say makes me feel any better. As we sit and talk about nothing at all, there's an ocean growing among us of all the things that are not being said.

The other dates with Abbott have been cancelled, but we don't talk about that.

I get the feeling that every one of them has a story of how they got here, and it is very similar to mine.

But none of us says a word about it.

This moment has the capacity to offer some hope. So, why dwell in the darkness?

Another round of elimination is coming up. Soon.

Mirabelle comes by and tells us.

What's going to happen there?

What more is in store for me?

And for the others?

I don't know.

But I don't have the energy to think about it anymore.

"Let's go for a swim," I suggest.

The girls look at me with surprise.

"C'mon, we have some time before we have to be there. It will be fun. We don't have enough fun."

The pool is calm and bright blue. It's calling my name.

I'm the first one out there and I dip my toe into the water out of habit. I was never the girl to just jump right in.

If the water is cold, I have to ready myself for it first. But this water is warm and comforting, the perfect temperature. I slide right into it.

When I come back up for air, the others are crowding around the edge.

The air is thick with humidity. Somewhere in the distance, a chorus of frogs is singing their hearts out. Teal and Savannah are smiling.

I dive under again and watch as my hair swirls around my head.

Despite everything that has happened, this is okay. No, more than okay.

Suddenly, for a brief moment, the reality of this place disappears.

Swimming around the pool, talking about

nothing at all and laughing, we are transformed into just a group of friends.

Fun.

Careless.

Free.

"It's time," Mirabelle says, walking up to us.

Just like that, it all vanishes.

CHAPTER 37 - EASTON

WHEN THERE'S ANOTHER ELIMINATION...

I couldn't find her. I searched for her everywhere and then Mirabelle told me that she was on a date with Abbott.

This wasn't part of the plan, but few things around here follow the plan.

Everyone was watching, but I couldn't.

He wasn't there to watch my dates, so I couldn't watch his. But York is the last place in the world to care about fairness.

I pace just outside the theater room, trying to figure out what to do.

The first date went fine. Cordial.

Nothing out of the ordinary.

But he wasn't on a date with Everly.

There's something about Everly that makes his whole body spit bile.

He has this anger and hatred for her that I've never seen before. Is it because *I* care about her?

I think about that for a moment. Perhaps.

What if all of these feelings that he has pointed at Everly are really directed at me?

Then suddenly, something goes wrong.

Mirabelle tells me to stay put, but takes a few guards into the dining room with her.

I try to follow them, but two large burly men physically stop me, blocking my entrance. I can't get through.

Time moves like molasses until Mirabelle emerges.

Two guards follow close behind, with Abbott in the middle.

His head is hanging low.

Somewhere in the distance, a girl about Everly's age is crying, sitting on the floor.

Everly is staring into space as if she's in a trance. Emotionless. Traumatized.

"What happened?" I roar and run to Abbott. "What did you do?"

They pull me away from him and out into the hallway.

Two men hold me back, but not before I land two punches.

One on his face and one in his stomach.

He reaches for me, but other guards grab his arms just before we collide.

Oh how I wish no one else was here.

I need to finish *this* once and for all.

IT'S time for an elimination again.

I sit in a small room with guards on the outside.

I have to cool off, they say.

I can't just attack Abbott like that, they say.

But what I'm really doing here is waiting for my father to make a decision as to what's going to happen next.

I attacked Abbott, but this act shouldn't be judged too harshly by my father, not in comparison to what Abbott did. Of course, our father is hardly predictable.

Through the grapevine, I hear bits and pieces of what happened on Everly's date.

He didn't touch her, but he made her watch. I guess it was some sort of promise of what's to come.

I go over my options.

The window is open and it's looking over the roof.

I could use it to climb down.

And then what?

Go where exactly? And what about Everly?

I have to wait and see.

IT'S TIME.

I walk out into the foyer following Mirabelle.

Abbott comes in after me.

The contestants are already standing in line, next to J. The panel of judges is on the other side.

What is their job exactly? I wonder. To observe and record and make recommendations to my father, ones he rarely listens to.

Abbott takes his position next to me. As he glares at me, his nostrils actually flare open with each breath.

I'm not fazed.

There was a time, a long time ago, when I was afraid of him.

But not anymore.

Now, I know his secret.

He does these things to others he perceives are weaker than him for only one reason.

He is a coward.

A narcissistic asshole without an empathetic feeling in his body.

"The King will be here shortly," J, the host, says.

No one responds.

I look over at Everly.

Her eyes meet mine, pleading for something.

She needs my help.

I give her a reassuring nod.

It's all going to be okay, I mouth slightly.

She nods back without much conviction.

"Okay then, I've heard that things aren't exactly going as planned," Father says as soon as he walks through the doorway.

No one responds.

"I thought that my sons would be able to show you girls a good time. But I guess not," he adds with a laugh.

Abbott looks down at the floor.

I doubt that he's sorry for what he did, but I have no doubt about the fact that he's sorry everyone found out about it.

"Anyway, I think this competition has dragged on far enough. It's supposed to be fun for all. And I can tell that it hasn't been that for a bit. So, why don't we all just end it right here and now?"

My father poses the question as if anyone here is in a position to disagree with him.

Again, no one says anything.

Father is milking the moment.

He lives for the time when everyone is hanging on what he's about to say next.

"As you may or may not know, my sons will be choosing their wives, first," Father says turning to the contestants. "J will explain it further."

"Yes, of course," J says, scrambling a little for the right words. "As I'm sure I've mentioned before, the Princes of York will be proposing first."

It is clear from the women's faces that none of this was mentioned before.

"And if you want to decline, you are, of course, welcome to," J adds. "Right, Your Majesty?"

"Yes, of course," Father says tossing his hands in the air to drive the point home. "What kind of place do you think we're running here?"

"Easton, let's start with you," he says turning to face me.

I look at him, raising my eyebrows.

I'm not entirely sure what he wants me to say.

"Is there someone here that you would like to propose to?" he asks, handing me a velvet box.

"Yes, of course," I say, taking the box. "I've enjoyed spending time with all of you, but there's only one with whom I really made a connection."

I look at her and smile. "Everly, will you please come up here?"

CHAPTER 38 - EASTON

WHEN IT'S HIS TURN...

*S*he walks up slowly, as if she isn't sure that this is really happening. When she's close enough, I get down on my knee.

"Will you marry me?" I ask.

Tears run down her face. Her whole body trembles and she whispers, "yes."

I open the box and place the large diamond ring on her finger.

It's bigger than the one I gave her before. I want to give her something more personal later, a ring that I pick out. But this will work for now.

Everly stares at the ring and wraps her arms around me. My father starts to clap and everyone follows along.

I have never asked anyone to marry me before.

I've never even been close.

Things are different with Everly. As a result of being here, as a result of our fleeting time together, our relationship has been sped up.

Accelerated.

The closeness that I feel toward her, it's like I'm...home.

Would I ask her to marry me if we had met under different circumstances?

Out there in the real world? Yes.

One-hundred times yes.

The proposal is required and yet it's real.

I have to pick someone. Yes, that part is true.

But I would've picked her anyway.

A small tear runs down her face.

I wipe it off. Another one follows quickly behind.

Out here, in front of everyone, it's hard to tell what is real and what is not.

She is afraid of my father, and Abbott, and she is relieved that I'm the one asking to marry her.

But does she really want to marry me?

Or is this an act on her part?

Does she think it's an act on mine?

"I love you, Everly," I whisper. "I always have. I always will."

She nods and says that she loves me, too.

I hear her words.

I want to believe her, but it's hard to know what's true and what's not.

"Why does Easton get to go first?" Abbott asks.

Everly reaches out for my hand and squeezes it tightly.

"What if I want her too?"

"You can't have her," Father says.

There's a finality in his voice. It gives me peace. "You should count yourself lucky that I'm letting you propose at all given what just happened."

Abbott shrugs and waves his hand as if he were untouchable. "Maybe I don't want a wife at all."

"That's not up to you."

"Why not?"

Father scowls at him. He does not like us talking back to him, let alone in front of company.

"But it's not fair," he wines. "I didn't even get to go on a date with all of them."

"That's because you misbehaved on your second one," Father snaps.

Abbott tenses his body and looks from one contestant to another.

Everly squeezes my hand in anticipation.

They all look forlorn and disappointed. After

what happened, I'm not sure any of them are hoping for a proposal from him. But what's the alternative?

"Fine," Father says interrupting the tense silence. "You will *not* get the privilege of their company. The proposal is off."

Everly looks up at me.

I am as much in the dark as she is.

Teal's eyes grow big with fear. I know what she's thinking; if none of them are chosen then they are all eliminated.

"What do you mean?" Abbott asks.

"The competition is over," Father says.

J and Mirabelle have the same perplexed expression on their faces as I probably do.

"This whole thing has been off since the beginning. Nothing feels right. If you don't want to ask any of these beautiful young ladies to marry you, that's your problem."

Father turns around to leave.

"So, what's going to happen?" Abbott asks.

"We're going to have a wedding for your brother and we are all going to be very happy for them."

I feel Everly let out a big sigh of relief. She lets go of my hand for a moment, but then clamps back on.

"Okay, ladies, you heard His Majesty. Your time

with us is over," J announces. Teal and Olivia gasp in fear. "I'm sorry, but you have been eliminated."

Quiet sobs and the flow of tears echo around the hall.

"Did I say that, you moron?" Father roars at J.

Savannah and Olivia look up at him, wiping their eyes with the back of their hands.

"I'm...sorry...I...just...assumed," J stumbles over his words.

"Didn't your mother teach you why you should never assume?"

J shakes his head.

"When you assume you make an ass out of *you* and *me*," Father says. "Get it?"

This is one of his favorite lessons. I've heard it at least a dozen times growing up.

"Why shouldn't you assume anything, J?" Father asks, to drive the point home.

J repeats the lesson and Father gives him a knowing smile.

"Ladies, you are *not* eliminated," he finally says. "Everly will need help in implementing her duties as the Princess of York. Since you all get along so well, I thought it would be nice if you stuck around and joined the court as her ladies in waiting."

They let out a communal sigh of relief.

More tears follow, but these are ones of joy.

Everly squeezes my hand again and flashes me a big smile. Then she runs over to Teal and the others and wraps her arms around them.

CHAPTER 39 - EVERLY

WHEN WE ARE ALONE...

I sit in Easton's living room and wait as he makes me dinner. He is just making us an omelet, but I know that it will be the best tasting omelets I've ever had.

I am to be his wife.

He proposed to me.

Me.

I glance up at him and wonder what I ever did to get this lucky.

We are alone now.

There are no cameras.

No one is watching.

"Can I ask you something?" I ask, trying to buy myself more time.

He nods, giving me a small smile out of the corner of his lips.

"Did you mean that?"

He looks up at me from the stove.

"Mean what?"

"The proposal?"

"Every word of it," he says.

I nod, still not completely sure if I believe him.

"It's just that I wasn't sure," I say. "I mean, I know you were glad this competition wasn't about your father anymore and you didn't want anything bad to happen to me. I totally understand why you did it. But we don't have to be married, if you don't want to."

My mind is running a mile a minute and I keep stumbling over my words. I don't know if it's all coming out right.

"What I mean is that I really appreciate you proposing to me. It was a noble thing to do. I know you did it to help me. But if you don't *really* want to be married, I totally understand. We don't have to be," I add. I'm not sure if this makes anything any clearer.

Easton moves the skillet off the burner and walks over to me. Sitting down in front of me, he takes my hand in his.

He stares at me for a long time before saying a word. Then he takes a deep breath.

"I've given that a lot of thought, Everly. I mean, yes, I want to help you. Of course. And yes, in similar circumstances, I would probably propose to any of the girls here if that's what it took to save their life."

I nod. That's what I thought, of course.

I'm so stupid.

He's just a very nice guy who thinks this place is as evil as I do.

"But the thing is, Everly, that when I stood there before you, I realized something," Easton continues. "When I asked you to marry me it's because I really do want to marry you. It's crazy, and rash, and probably wrong, but I love you and I want to spend the rest of my life with you. I want you to be my wife."

The words come out of left field.

I don't expect them at all and they actually take my breath away.

"Say something," he says.

"I...don't..." I start to speak without knowing where to go.

"Please don't feel like you have to say the same thing back to me. I know that your time here hasn't been perfect. Far from it. I don't want to put any more pressure on you. I just want you to know how I feel. That's it."

Finally, my thoughts come into focus.

"I love you, Easton," I say. "I know that I probably shouldn't. I know that it's not a smart thing to do here. But I do. And when you asked me to marry you...it felt so...real. It felt like there was no one else in the room and that it was just you and me."

He runs his finger along my lips and then presses his lips onto mine. I kiss him back. Burying his hands in my hair, he tugs at it slightly. I moan and tilt my head back, exposing my neck to him.

Our bodies are more familiar with each other now.

We know each other's movements.

We know what to expect.

And yet, something about his touch still takes my breath away.

As he stands next to me, I inhale his scent.

He smells of power, and strength, and comfort all at the same time. As he runs his hand down my back, a tingling sensation spreads through me, starting from somewhere deep inside. I tense my legs to keep it at bay, but it's here to stay.

He brings his lips closer to mine again, but this time we do not touch.

Instead, we stand so close together that I can feel his breath on my lips. I reach for him, but he holds me back. He holds my head in his hands and doesn't let me get any closer. That's when I reach out my tongue and run it along his lower lip.

"Hmm," he says. "Sneaky! Sneaky!"

I nod and break out of his grasp. I press my lips onto his and wait for him to kiss me back.

When I pull away, I see his eyes darken and turn almost smoky in their gaze.

"Oh is that what you want?" Easton asks, grabbing me by my shoulders. I look up at him surprised.

"You want it rough?" He asks.

His hands press into my shoulders and the warmth in between my legs gets hotter.

"Maybe," I say, giving him a slight nod.

Without another word, he grabs me by my arm and pushes me into the bedroom where the lights are dimmed low.

"Wait," he says and I stand perfectly still in the twilight.

He lights four candles, slowly and deliberately.

Then he walks back up to me.

"Take off your clothes," he says.

I like the command in his voice.

I like the directness.

In a world that I'm always trying to influence, it is nice to give up control for once - *give it up to someone I trust with my body and soul.*

"Are you going to do it or do you want me to do it for you?" He asks.

CHAPTER 40 - EVERLY

THAT NIGHT...

I smile a little out of the corner of my mouth and do as he says.

This is a new side of him. It's an unexpected one. It scares me, but in that good way.

I pull my shirt over my head and then peel off my leggings.

"All of it," he says, and I unclasp my bra.

My breasts fall open before him.

When I reach for my panties, he stops me.

"Not yet," he says.

"Go sit there," he points to the leather sofa-like chair to the right of the King-size bed.

I do as he says.

"Open your legs and put them on the arms of the chair."

Again, I do as I am told. I'm scared, but it's a good kind of fear. I'm about to ride a rollercoaster. I know that I'm going to make it to the end in one piece, I just don't know how.

Easton takes off his shirt and unbuckles his belt.

He slides his pants off and steps out of them.

His chiseled body sizzles in the candlelight and it takes all of my strength to *not* reach out for him.

Easton is dressed in a pair of James Bond boxer-briefs. Tight and black, exposing exactly how big his package is without showing it off completely.

"Now, don't remove your hands from the arm rests, no matter what," Easton says. "Or there will be consequences."

I nod and lick my lips in anticipation.

He kneels down before me.

He slides my panties to the side, exposing me.

Wet and thirsty for him, he touches my yearning.

He makes his way carefully around the lace, toying with me.

Flirting with me.

Touching me in every way that I want and have to be touched.

Opening me up wide, he finally presses his lips to me and pushes his fingers deep inside.

I moan and say his name over and over again.

He continues without stopping.

Small swirls become bigger and stronger ones. He opens me up wider and wider until his hand and mouth are glistening wet with my arousal.

As his mouth makes its way toward my clit and makes a home there, one of his fingers wanders toward my butt. It's surprising at first, but also good.

Really good.

He plays with my butt cheeks, squeezing and tugging prior to pressing his finger inside. I feel myself tightening up and then slowly letting him further inside.

"Oh Easton," I moan, arching my back, when his thrusts get stronger and stronger.

"You can't come until I say so," he says, pulling away from me for a moment.

But it's too late.

Pleasure starts to pulse through my body without my control.

Everything tightens around his fingers and then lets go completely.

My toes point outward and my body beings to shake.

He continues to thrust his fingers in and out of me for the duration until I collapse limply into the chair, completely spent.

"You are a very bad girl," Easton says, pulling away from me and licking his fingers.

"I'm sorry," I say without meaning a word of it.

"You should not have done that," he says, adjusting my panties back in place.

I put my feet to the ground. The hardwood floor feels cold and nice on my bare feet, still tingling from everything that has happened.

"Why? What do you mean?" I ask.

My body is spent, but new desire for him is starting to build up.

"I told you you couldn't and you still did it," Easton says. "Now, you're going to have to pay the price."

* * *

My whole body pulsates with anticipation. Easton is going to punish me and I can't wait to find out what he has in mind.

I trust him. I love him.

And that's what makes this so...delicious.

Easton leans over me. He pulls my hair back and gives me a kiss.

Only this time, the kiss is completely different from the ones before.

His tongue isn't softly brushing against mine. No, he is no longer asking permission. He is taking what's his.

He presses his lips onto mine and pushes his tongue inside. It swirls around mine for only a brief second before making its way down my neck and toward my breasts.

He explores my body like I belong to him. He demands that I let him as if I don't have a choice.

Every part of me is screaming yes. My heart starts to pound faster and faster and his hands make their way around me. His teeth find my nipples and bite down. The pain is a good kind of pain that makes me even wetter than I am already. My legs open up on their own.

Easton pulls me to the bed.

When he is about to flip me over, I stop him.

I reach for him and put him in my mouth. His hands scoop my hair and he gives out a loud moan. I run my tongue around him and pick up the pace.

His fingers tighten around my hair, tugging at it along with each of my movements. His hips move toward and away from me as he continues to moan with satisfaction.

The louder he is and the stronger his thrusts get, the more tightness I feel in my core. I squeeze my thighs together and feel the warmth in between my legs. It's the start of another explosion, the beginning of the build.

Just when I feel him getting close, he pulls out. Grabbing me by the back of my neck, he flips me over and leans me over the mattress.

"Don't move," he says and I give myself over to him.

After giving me one long kiss down there, he spreads my legs with his hands and positions himself behind me.

"You're so beautiful," he says, running his hands up and down my back.

I arch my body toward him.

I feel myself opening wide for him.

My body is begging for him to come inside.

Easton grabs onto my hips. I feel him throbbing impatiently and then he slips right in. Placing his hand on my shoulder to steady himself, he starts to move in and out of me.

The movements are slow at first.

Deliberate.

But they quickly accelerate, turning into short quick thrusts. Just as before, we morph into one being.

I can no longer tell where my body ends and his

begins. Our love-making becomes a dance. His hands lose their way around me as his lips kiss my neck and back with abandon.

A warm sensation starts to build deep inside.

I don't have the strength to keep it at bay or to slow it down.

He is doing beautiful things to me and my body is no longer my own.

I yell his name as a wave pulsates through me, starting at my core. Holding me closer, he moves in and out of me even faster until one final thrust.

A moment later, completely spent, we collapse into each other's arms.

CHAPTER 41 - EVERLY

LATER THAT NIGHT...

*A*s we lie in the afterglow of what just happened, the world suddenly doesn't seem so bad. I have a man I love who loves me back. I don't want to make a life with him *here*, but I know that I want to make a life with him.

"Have you given any more thought to what we talked about before?" I ask.

I don't want to mention Dagger or his father or Alicia.

No one is supposed to be listening, but how do I know that for sure?

I almost divulged that information to the whole world before, I will not make the same mistake twice.

"You mean about how I tried to leave before?" he whispers.

I suspect that he has the same suspicions as I do.

I give Easton a small nod.

"I don't know," he says. "I haven't made any plans yet."

"So, what do you think is going to happen now? I mean with us and the wedding?"

Easton shrugs and sits up a bit in bed. "If my father has his way, which he will, it will likely be a grand affair. Lots of invitations to lots of important people. Your parents, of course."

"My parents?" I ask in a gasp.

The thought had never occurred to me.

"Yes," he nods. "It's a real wedding. Your side of the family. My side of the family. At least, that's what I suspect."

"And if I were marrying your father?" I ask.

"Then it would've been a little different," he says. "I'm not sure if your parents would've been invited. But this is...a real wedding. I mean, he's pretty serious about wanting me to find someone I want to marry. Have kids with."

I sit up in bed. That phrase, *have kids with*, just hangs in the air between us.

"Do you *not* want kids?" Easton asks.

"I haven't really thought about it," I say after a moment.

What I really want to say is that yes, of course, I do.

But no, not yet.

And not under these circumstances. But again, I bite my tongue.

This place is supposed to be safe now.

The competition is over.

We are alone, but are we really?

I mean, can I tell Easton what I really think without consequences from the higher ups?

I decide to take the conversation in a different direction.

"So...where will we live after the wedding?" I ask.

"Come with me," Easton says.

He pulls me from out of the covers and toward the bathroom. There, he pulls down the sheet that I wrapped around myself, and leads me into the shower. When the water starts to run over us, he leans closer to me.

"This is just a precaution," he whispers.

I nod.

"We are not staying here. I'm going to marry you and take you away from here."

"And they will just...let us leave?" I ask.

"I think so. I don't live here. My life and my job are in Manhattan. I'd like to go back there...with you."

I nod.

Suddenly, I can't see a thing through the tears streaming down my face and the hot water gushing out of the shower head. I begin to sob.

"Are you okay?" Easton asks, wrapping his arms around me.

I mumble something incoherent in response.

He brings me closer and holds me tighter.

"We are going to get out of here, Everly," he whispers.

"But what about...what you said before?" I ask quietly. "About Dagger and your father?"

The last bit is inaudible, so Easton reads my lips.

"I've given that a lot of thought," he says after a moment. "The thing about revenge is that it can consume you, you know? It can take over your life. And now that I have this opportunity, to marry you and be with you forever, I don't want to do anything to jeopardize that. At least, not now."

I nod.

"If my father is willing to leave us alone, then why shouldn't we take him up on that?"

I nod again.

He's right.

Of course, he's right.

I mean, I've vowed revenge myself.

There are a lot of things I want to get payback for - everything that happened to me in the dungeon, for one.

But how can I do that *and* get out of this place in one piece?

Is that even possible?

No, perhaps, marrying Easton is my best bet.

I love him.

I would marry him anyway, despite his family. And if after the wedding they allow us to start our lives together somewhere else...why press our luck? Why fight a losing battle?

"I agree with you," I say after a moment. "There's no reason to create conflict when your father is willing to give us everything we want."

Easton gives me a smile and a peck on the head.

I exhale deeply.

We stand there under the strong flow of hot water, holding onto each other.

Everything is going to be okay now, I say to myself.

You can relax.

Everything is going to be fine.

When I look up at Easton again, he kneels down and kisses me.

His lips feel like home now.

Soft and knowing.

I kiss him back.

His hands make their way down my breasts and my fingers dig into his strong, broad shoulders.

He kneels down before me and runs his hands down my stomach.

I spread my legs, welcoming his mouth.

A loud knock startles me.

The bathroom door swings open and four guards in black uniforms come in. Easton scrambles up to his feet.

"What the hell—" he starts to say.

One of the guards opens the glass door, reaches in and physically pulls him out of the shower.

I try to stop him, but the others point their guns in my face and scream at me until I throw my arms in the air.

"Get off me!" he roars. "Do you know who I am?"

"Easton Bay, Prince of York, you are under arrest for the murder of Christopher Weider," the guard says. "You have the right to remain silent. Everything you say will be used against you. You have the right to an attorney..."

Easton begins to shout at them, but the guard continues to read him his rights. It takes all four of them to extract him from the room.

I turn off the water, grab a towel and run after them.

Mirabelle meets me at the top of the stairs and blocks my exit.

"What is going on? Where are they taking him? He didn't kill anyone!" I scream.

Mirabelle shakes her head, looking distant and tired.

"Who is Christopher Weider?" I ask, in a more calm and collected tone. "Easton didn't kill anyone. Don't they know that?"

"Yes, he did," Mirabelle whispers.

I shake my head and repeat the word *no* over and over again.

"Christopher Weider's nickname is Dagger, Everly. Easton killed him to avenge the death of his ex, Alicia."

I shake my head and take a step back toward the wall.

Quickly, my legs give out and I slide all the way to the ground.

No.

No.

No.

He didn't do this.

Mirabelle gets down on the floor and wraps her arms around me.

"I'm so sorry, Everly," she whispers. I turn around and bury my face in her shoulder.

"He didn't kill Dagger. He was starting a new life with me," I mumble over and over.

"There is no point to revenge. That's what he said to me. That's what he promised me," I whisper.

Nodding her head, Mirabelle wraps her arms around me and holds me.

I want to run after him, to demand more answers.

But I can't.

My body goes limp.

He couldn't have killed him, I say to myself. He said that there was no point to revenge. He said that if his father were willing to let us start our life together, why would he jeopardize it?

And then something occurs to me.

Did he say all that because Dagger was dead already?

THANK you for reading CROWN OF YORK!

I hope you are enjoying Everly and Easton's story. It continues. **One-click THRONE OF YORK Now!**

I don't know who to believe, but I know that this place is full of lies secrets.

Easton Bay has risked everything to protect me, but that doesn't mean that he did not do what they say he did.

I am in love with him. **I am supposed to be his wife, but this changes everything.** The King has turned on him. I'm Easton's only hope.

But it's only a matter of time before they turns on me, too.

Is my fate is sealed?

One-click THRONE OF YORK Now!

CAN'T WAIT for Throne of York to come out?

Want to read a "Decadent, delicious, & dangerously addictive!" romance you will not be able to put down? **1-Click Black Edge NOW!**

I DON'T BELONG HERE.

I'm in way over my head. But I have debts to pay.

They call my name. The spotlight is on. The auction starts.

Mr. Black is the highest bidder. He's dark, rich, and powerful. He likes to play games.

The only rule is there are no rules.

But it's just one night. **What's the worst that can happen?**

1-Click BLACK EDGE Now!

START READING BLACK EDGE ON THE NEXT PAGE!

CHAPTER 1- ELLIE

WHEN THE INVITATION ARRIVES...

"*H*ere it is! Here it is!" my roommate Caroline yells at the top of her lungs as she runs into my room.

We were friends all through Yale and we moved to New York together after graduation.

Even though I've known Caroline for what feels like a million years, I am still shocked by the exuberance of her voice. It's quite loud given the smallness of her body.

Caroline is one of those super skinny girls who can eat pretty much anything without gaining a pound.

Unfortunately, I am not that talented. In fact, my body seems to have the opposite gift. I can eat nothing but vegetables for a week straight, eat one slice of pizza, and gain a pound.

"What is it?" I ask, forcing myself to sit up.

It's noon and I'm still in bed.

My mother thinks I'm depressed and wants me to see her shrink.

She might be right, but I can't fathom the strength.

"The invitation!" Caroline says jumping in bed next to me.

I stare at her blankly.

And then suddenly it hits me.

This must be *the* invitation.

"You mean...it's..."

"Yes!" she screams and hugs me with excitement.

"Oh my God!" She gasps for air and pulls away from me almost as quickly.

"Hey, you know I didn't brush my teeth yet," I say turning my face away from hers.

"Well, what are you waiting for? Go brush them," she instructs.

Begrudgingly, I make my way to the bathroom.

We have been waiting for this invitation for some time now.

And by we, I mean Caroline.

I've just been playing along, pretending to care, not really expecting it to show up.

Without being able to contain her excitement, Caroline bursts through the door when my mouth is still full of toothpaste.

She's jumping up and down, holding a box in her hand.

"Wait, what's that?" I mumble and wash my mouth out with water.

"This is it!" Caroline screeches and pulls me into the living room before I have a chance to wipe my mouth with a towel.

"But it's a box," I say staring at her.

"Okay, okay," Caroline takes a couple of deep yoga breaths, exhaling loudly.

She puts the box carefully on our dining room table. There's no address on it.

It looks something like a fancy gift box with a big monogrammed C in the middle.

Is the C for Caroline?

"Is this how it came? There's no address on it?" I ask.

"It was hand-delivered," Caroline whispers.

I hold my breath as she carefully removes the top part, revealing the satin and silk covered wood box inside.

The top of it is gold plated with whimsical twirls all around the edges, and the mirrored area is engraved with her full name.

Caroline Elizabeth Kennedy Spruce.

Underneath her name is a date, one week in the future. 8 PM.

We stare at it for a few moments until Caroline reaches for the elegant knob to open the box.

Inside, Caroline finds a custom monogram made of foil in gold on silk emblazoned on the inside of the flap cover.

There's also a folio covered in silk. Caroline carefully opens the folio and finds another foil monogram and the invitation.

The inside invitation is one layer, shimmer white, with gold writing.

"Is this for real? How many layers of invitation are there?" I ask.

But the presentation is definitely doing its job. We are both duly impressed.

"There's another knob," I say, pointing to the knob in front of the box.

I'm not sure how we had missed it before.

Caroline carefully pulls on this knob, revealing a drawer that holds the inserts (a card with directions and a response card).

"Oh my God, I can't go to this alone," Caroline mumbles, turning to me.

I stare blankly at her.

Getting invited to this party has been her dream ever since she found out about it from someone in the Cicada 17, a super-secret society at Yale.

"Look, here, it says that I can bring a friend," she yells out even though I'm standing right next to her.

"It probably says a date. A plus one?" I say.

"No, a friend. Girl preferred," Caroline reads off the invitation card.

That part of the invitation is in very small ink, as if someone made the person stick it on, without their express permission.

"I don't want to crash," I say.

Frankly, I don't really want to go.

These kind of upper-class events always make me feel a little bit uncomfortable.

"Hey, aren't you supposed to be at work?" I ask.

"Eh, I took a day off," Caroline says waving her arm. "I knew that the invitation would come today and I just couldn't deal with work. You know how it is."

I nod. Sort of.

Caroline and I seem like we come from the same world.

We both graduated from private school, we both went to Yale, and our parents belong to the same exclusive country club in Greenwich, Connecticut.

But we're not really that alike.

Caroline's family has had money for many generations going back to the railroads.

My parents were an average middle class family from Connecticut.

They were both teachers and our idea of summering was renting a 1-bedroom bungalow near Clearwater, FL for a week.

But then my parents got divorced when I was 8, and my mother started tutoring kids to make extra money.

The pay was the best in Greenwich, where parents paid more than $100 an hour.

And that's how she met, Mitch Willoughby, my stepfather.

He was a widower with a five-year old daughter who was not doing well after her mom's untimely death.

Even though Mom didn't usually tutor anyone younger than 12, she agreed to take a meeting with Mitch and his daughter because $200 an hour was too much to turn down.

Three months later, they were in love and six

months later, he asked her to marry him on top of the Eiffel Tower.

They got married, when I was 11, in a huge 450-person ceremony in Nantucket.

So even though Caroline and I run in the same circles, we're not really from the same circle.

It has nothing to do with her, she's totally accepting, it's me.

I don't always feel like I belong.

Caroline majored in art-history at Yale, and she now works at an exclusive contemporary art gallery in Soho.

It's chic and tiny, featuring only 3 pieces of art at a time.

Ash, the owner - I'm not sure if that's her first or last name - mainly keeps the space as a showcase. What the gallery really specializes in is going to wealthy people's homes and choosing their art for them.

They're basically interior designers, but only for art.

None of the pieces sell for anything less than $200 grand, but Caroline's take home salary is about $21,000.

Clearly, not enough to pay for our 2 bedroom apartment in Chelsea.

Her parents cover her part of the rent and pay all of her other expenses.

Mine do too, of course.

Well, Mitch does.

I only make about $27,000 at my writer's assistant job and that's obviously not covering my half of our $6,000 per month apartment.

So, what's the difference between me and Caroline?

I guess the only difference is that I feel bad about taking the money.

I have a $150,000 school loan from Yale that I don't want Mitch to pay for.

It's my loan and I'm going to pay for it myself, dammit.

Plus, unlike Caroline, I know that real people don't really live like this.

Real people like my dad, who is being pressured to sell the house for more than a million dollars that he and my mom bought back in the late 80's (the neighborhood has gone up in price and teachers now have to make way for tech entrepreneurs and real estate moguls).

"How can you just not go to work like that? Didn't you use all of your sick days flying to Costa Rica last month?" I ask.

"Eh, who cares? Ash totally understands. Besides, she totally owes me. If it weren't for me, she would've never closed that geek millionaire who had the hots for me and ended up buying close to a million dollars' worth of art for his new mansion."

Caroline does have a way with men.

She's fun and outgoing and perky.

The trick, she once told me, is to figure out exactly what the guy wants to hear.

Because a geek millionaire, as she calls anyone who has made money in tech, does not want to hear the same thing that a football player wants to hear.

And neither of them want to hear what a trust fund playboy wants to hear.

But Caroline isn't a gold digger.

Not at all.

Her family owns half the East Coast.

And when it comes to men, she just likes to have fun.

I look at the time.

It's my day off, but that doesn't mean that I want to spend it in bed in my pajamas, listening to Caroline obsessing over what she's going to wear.

No, today, is my day to actually get some writing done.

I'm going to Starbucks, getting a table in the

back, near the bathroom, and am actually going to finish this short story that I've been working on for a month.

Or maybe start a new one.

I go to my room and start getting dressed.

I have to wear something comfortable, but something that's not exactly work clothes.

I hate how all of my clothes have suddenly become work clothes. It's like they've been tainted.

They remind me of work and I can't wear them out anymore on any other occasion. I'm not a big fan of my work, if you can't tell.

Caroline follows me into my room and plops down on my bed.

I take off my pajamas and pull on a pair of leggings.

Ever since these have become the trend, I find myself struggling to force myself into a pair of jeans.

They're just so comfortable!

"Okay, I've come to a decision," Caroline says. "You *have* to come with me!"

"Oh, I have to come with you?" I ask, incredulously. "Yeah, no, I don't think so."

"Oh c'mon! Please! Pretty please! It will be so much fun!"

"Actually, you can't make any of those promises.

You have no idea what it will be," I say, putting on a long sleeve shirt and a sweater with a zipper in the front.

Layers are important during this time of year.

The leaves are changing colors, winds are picking up, and you never know if it's going to be one of those gorgeous warm, crisp New York days they like to feature in all those romantic comedies or a soggy, overcast dreary day that only shows up in one scene at the end when the two main characters fight or break up (but before they get back together again).

"Okay, yes, I see your point," Caroline says, sitting up and crossing her legs. "But here is what we *do* know. We do know that it's going to be amazing. I mean, look at the invitation. It's a freakin' box with engravings and everything!"

Usually, Caroline is much more eloquent and better at expressing herself.

"Okay, yes, the invitation is impressive," I admit.

"And as you know, the invitation is everything. I mean, it really sets the mood for the party. The event! And not just the mood. It establishes a certain expectation. And this box..."

"Yes, the invitation definitely sets up a certain expectation," I agree.

"So?"

"So?" I ask her back.

"Don't you want to find out what that expectation is?"

"No." I shake my head categorically.

"Okay. So what else do we know?" Caroline asks rhetorically as I pack away my Mac into my bag.

"I have to go, Caroline," I say.

"No, listen. The yacht. Of course, the yacht. How could I bury the lead like that?" She jumps up and down with excitement again.

"We also know that it's going to be this super exclusive event on a *yacht*! And not just some small 100 footer, but a *mega*-yacht."

I stare at her blankly, pretending to not be impressed.

When Caroline first found out about this party, through her ex-boyfriend, we spent days trying to figure out what made this event so special.

But given that neither of us have been on a yacht before, at least not a mega-yacht – we couldn't quite get it.

"You know the yacht is going to be amazing!"

"Yes, of course," I give in. "But that's why I'm sure that you're going to have a wonderful time by yourself. I have to go."

I grab my keys and toss them into the bag.

"Ellie," Caroline says.

The tone of her voice suddenly gets very serious, to match the grave expression on her face.

"Ellie, please. I don't think I can go by myself."

CHAPTER 2 - ELLIE

WHEN YOU HAVE COFFEE WITH A GUY YOU CAN'T HAVE...

*A*nd that's pretty much how I was roped into going.

You don't know Caroline, but if you did, the first thing you'd find out is that she is not one to take things seriously.

Nothing fazes her.

Nothing worries her.

Sometimes she is the most enlightened person on earth, other times she's the densest.

Most of the time, I'm jealous of the fact that she simply lives life in the present.

"So, you're going?" my friend Tom asks.

He brought me my pumpkin spice latte, the first one of the season!

I close my eyes and inhale it's sweet aroma before taking the first sip.

But even before its wonderful taste of cinnamon and nutmeg runs down my throat, Tom is already criticizing my decision.

"I can't believe you're actually going," he says.

"Oh my God, now I know it's officially fall," I change the subject.

"Was there actually such a thing as autumn before the pumpkin spice latte? I mean, I remember that we had falling leaves, changing colors, all that jazz, but without this...it's like Christmas without a Christmas tree."

"Ellie, it's a day after Labor Day," Tom rolls his eyes. "It's not fall yet."

I take another sip. "Oh yes, I do believe it is."

"Stop changing the subject," Tom takes a sip of his plain black coffee.

How he doesn't get bored with that thing, I'll never know.

But that's the thing about Tom.

He's reliable.

Always on time, never late.

It's nice. That's what I have always liked about him.

He's basically the opposite of Caroline in every way.

And that's what makes seeing him like this, as only a friend, so hard.

"Why are you going there? Can't Caroline go by herself?" Tom asks, looking straight into my eyes.

His hair has this annoying tendency of falling into his face just as he's making a point – as a way of accentuating it.

It's actually quite vexing especially given how irresistible it makes him look.

His eyes twinkle under the low light in the back of the Starbucks.

"I'm going as her plus one," I announce.

I make my voice extra perky on purpose.

So that it portrays excitement, rather than apprehensiveness, which is actually how I'm feeling over the whole thing.

"She's making you go as her plus one," Tom announces as a matter a fact. He knows me too well.

"I just don't get it, Ellie. I mean, why bother? It's a super yacht filled with filthy rich people. I mean, how fun can that party be?"

"Jealous much?" I ask.

"I'm not jealous at all!" He jumps back in his seat. "If that's what you think…"

He lets his words trail off and suddenly the conversation takes on a more serious mood.

"You don't have to worry, I'm not going to miss your engagement party," I say quietly. It's the weekend after I get back."

He shakes his head and insists that that's not what he's worried about.

"I just don't get it Ellie," he says.

You don't get it?

You don't get why I'm going?

I've had feelings for you for, what, two years now?

But the time was never right.

At first, I was with my boyfriend and the night of our breakup, you decided to kiss me.

You totally caught me off guard.

And after that long painful breakup, I wasn't ready for a relationship.

And you, my best friend, you weren't really a rebound contender.

And then, just as I was about to tell you how I felt, you spend the night with Carrie.

Beautiful, wealthy, witty Carrie. Carrie Warrenhouse, the current editor of BuzzPost, the online magazine where we both work, and the daughter of Edward Warrenhouse, the owner of

BuzzPost.

Oh yeah, and on top of all that, you also started seeing her and then asked her to marry you.

And now you two are getting married on Valentine's Day.

And I'm really happy for you.

Really.

Truly.

The only problem is that I'm also in love with you.

And now, I don't know what the hell to do with all of this except get away from New York.

Even if it's just for a few days.

But of course, I can't say any of these things.

Especially the last part.

"This hasn't been the best summer," I say after a few moments. "And I just want to do something fun. Get out of town. Go to a party. Because that's all this is, a party."

"That's not what I heard," Tom says.

"What do you mean?"

"Ever since you told me you were going, I started looking into this event.

And the rumor is that it's not what it is."

I shake my head, roll my eyes.

"What? You don't believe me?" Tom asks incredulously.

I shake my head.

"Okay, what? What did you hear?"

"It's basically like a Playboy Mansion party on steroids. It's totally out of control. Like one big orgy."

"And you would know what a Playboy Mansion party is like," I joke.

"I'm being serious, Ellie. I'm not sure this is a good place for you. I mean, you're not Caroline."

"And what the hell does that mean?" I ask.

Now, I'm actually insulted.

At first, I was just listening because I thought he was being protective.

But now...

"What you don't think I'm fun enough? You don't think I like to have a good time?" I ask.

"That's not what I meant," Tom backtracks. I start to gather my stuff. "What are you doing?"

"No, you know what," I stop packing up my stuff. "I'm not leaving. You're leaving."

"Why?"

"Because I came here to write. I have work to do. I staked out this table and I'm not leaving until I have something written. I thought you wanted to have coffee with me. I thought we were friends. I didn't realize that you came here to chastise me about my decisions."

"That's not what I'm doing," Tom says, without getting out of his chair.

"You have to leave Tom. I want you to leave."

"I just don't understand what happened to us," he says getting up, reluctantly.

I stare at him as if he has lost his mind.

"You have no right to tell me what I can or can't do. You don't even have the right to tell your fiancée. Unless you don't want her to stay your fiancée for long."

"I'm not trying to tell you what to do, Ellie. I'm just worried. This super exclusive party on some mega-yacht, that's not you. That's not us."

"Not us? You've got to be kidding," I shake my head. "You graduated from Princeton, Tom. Your father is an attorney at one of the most prestigious law-firms in Boston. He has argued cases before the Supreme Court. You're going to marry the heir to the Warrenhouse fortune. I'm so sick and tired of your working class hero attitude, I can't even tell you. Now, are you going to leave or should I?"

The disappointment that I saw in Tom's eyes hurt me to my very soul.

But he had hurt me.

His engagement came completely out of left field.

I had asked him to give me some time after my breakup and after waiting for only two months, he started dating Carrie.

And then they moved in together. And then he asked her to marry him.

And throughout all that, he just sort of pretended that we were still friends.

Just like none of this ever happened.

I open my computer and stare at the half written story before me.

Earlier today, before Caroline, before Tom, I had all of these ideas.

I just couldn't wait to get started.

But now...I doubted that I could even spell my name right.

Staring at a non-moving blinker never fuels the writing juices.

I close my computer and look around the place.

All around me, people are laughing and talking.

Leggings and Uggs are back in season – even though the days are still warm and crispy.

It hasn't rained in close to a week and everyone's

good mood seems to be energized by the bright rays of the afternoon sun.

Last spring, I was certain that Tom and I would get together over the summer and I would spend the fall falling in love with my best friend.

And now?

Now, he's engaged to someone else.

Not just someone else – my boss!

And we just had a fight over some stupid party that I don't even really want to go to.

He's right, of course.

It's not my style.

My family might have money, but that's not the world in which I'm comfortable.

I'm always standing on the sidelines and it's not going to be any different at this party.

But if I don't go now, after this, that means that I'm listening to him.

And he has no right to tell me what to do.

So, I have to go.

How did everything get so messed up?

CHAPTER 3 - ELLIE

WHEN YOU GO SHOPPING FOR THE PARTY OF A LIFETIME...

"*W*hat the hell are you still doing hanging out with that asshole?" Caroline asks dismissively.

We are in Elle's, a small boutique in Soho, where you can shop by appointment only.

I didn't even know these places existed until Caroline introduced me to the concept.

Caroline is not a fan of Tom.

They never got along, not since he called her an East Side snob at our junior year Christmas party at Yale and she called him a middle class poseur.

Neither insult was very creative, but their insults got better over the years as their hatred for each other grew.

You know how in the movies, two characters who

hate each other in the beginning always end up falling in love by the end?

Well, for a while, I actually thought that would happen to them.

If not fall in love, at least hook up. But no, they stayed steadfast in their hatred.

"That guy is such a tool. I mean, who the hell is he to tell you what to do anyway? It's not like you're his girlfriend," Caroline says placing a silver beaded bandage dress to her body and extending her right leg in front.

Caroline is definitely a knock out.

She's 5'10", 125 pounds with legs that go up to her chin.

In fact, from far away, she seems to be all blonde hair and legs and nothing else.

"I think he was just concerned, given all the stuff that is out there about this party."

"Okay, first of all, you have to stop calling it a party."

"Why? What is it?"

"It's not a party. It's like calling a wedding a party. Is it a party? Yes. But is it bigger than that."

"I had no idea that you were so sensitive to language. Fine. What do you want me to call it?'

"An experience," she announces, completely seriously.

"Are you kidding me? No way. There's no way I'm going to call it an experience."

We browse in silence for a few moments.

Some of the dresses and tops and shoes are pretty, some aren't.

I'm the first to admit that I do not have the vocabulary or knowledge to appreciate a place like this.

Now, Caroline on the other hand...

"Oh my God, I'm just in love with all these one of a kind pieces you have here," she says to the woman upfront who immediately starts to beam with pride.

"That's what we're going for."

"These statement bags and the detailing on these booties – agh! To die for, right?" Caroline says and they both turn to me.

"Yeah, totally," I agree blindly.

"And these high-end core pieces, I could just wear this every day!" Caroline pulls up a rather structured cream colored short sleeve shirt with a tassel hem and a boxy fit.

I'm not sure what makes that shirt a so-called core piece, but I go with the flow.

I'm out of my element and I know it.

"Okay, so what are we supposed to wear to this *experience* if we don't even know what's going to be going on there."

"I'm not exactly sure but definitely not jeans and t-shirts," Caroline says referring to my staple outfit. "But the invitation also said not to worry. They have all the necessities if we forget something."

As I continue to aimlessly browse, my mind starts to wander.

And goes back to Tom.

I met Tom at the Harvard-Yale game.

He was my roommate's boyfriend's high school best friend and he came up for the weekend to visit him.

We became friends immediately.

One smile from him, even on Skype, made all of my worries disappear.

He just sort of got me, the way no one really did.

After graduation, we applied to work a million different online magazines and news outlets, but BuzzPost was the one place that took both of us.

We didn't exactly plan to end up at the same place, but it was a nice coincidence.

He even asked if I wanted to be his roommate – but I had already agreed to room with Caroline.

He ended up in this crappy fourth floor walkup

in Hell's Kitchen – one of the only buildings that they haven't gentrified yet.

So, the rent was still somewhat affordable. Like I said, Tom likes to think of himself as a working class hero even though his upbringing is far from it.

Whenever he came over to our place, he always made fun of how expensive the place was, but it was always in good fun.

At least, it felt like it at the time.

Now?

I'm not so sure anymore.

"Do you think that Tom is really going to get married?" I ask Caroline while we're changing.

She swings my curtain open in front of the whole store.

I'm topless, but luckily I'm facing away from her and the assistant is buried in her phone.

"What are you doing?" I shriek and pull the curtain closed.

"What are you thinking?" she demands.

I manage to grab a shirt and cover myself before Caroline pulls the curtain open again.

She is standing before me in only a bra and a matching pair of panties – completely confident and unapologetic.

I think she's my spirit animal.

"Who cares about Tom?" Caroline demands.

"I do," I say meekly.

"Well, you shouldn't. He's a dick. You are way too good for him. I don't even understand what you see in him."

"He's my friend," I say as if that explains everything.

Caroline knows how long I've been in love with Tom.

She knows everything.

At times, I wish I hadn't been so open.

But other times, it's nice to have someone to talk to.

Even if she isn't exactly understanding.

"You can't just go around pining for him, Ellie. You can do so much better than him. You were with your ex and he just hung around waiting and waiting. Never telling you how he felt. Never making any grand gestures."

Caroline is big on gestures.

The grander the better.

She watches a lot of movies and she demands them of her dates.

And the funny thing is that you often get exactly what you ask from the world.

"I don't care about that," I say. "We were in the wrong place for each other.

I was with someone and then I wasn't ready to jump into another relationship right away.

And then...he and Carrie got together."

"There's no such thing as not the right time. Life is what you make it, Ellie. You're in control of your life. And I hate the fact that you're acting like you're not the main character in your own movie."

"I don't even know what you're talking about," I say.

"All I'm saying is that you deserve someone who tells you how he feels. Someone who isn't afraid of rejection. Someone who isn't afraid to put it all out there."

"Maybe that's who you want," I say.

"And that's not who you want?" Caroline says taking a step back away from me.

I think about it for a moment.

"Well, no I wouldn't say that. It is who I want," I finally say. "But I had a boyfriend then. And Tom and I were friends. So I couldn't expect him to—"

"You couldn't expect him to put it all out there? Tell you how he feels and take the risk of getting hurt?" Caroline cuts me off.

I hate to admit it, but that's exactly what I want.

That's exactly what I wanted from him back then.

I didn't want him to just hang around being my friend, making me question my feelings for him.

And if he had done that, if he had told me how he felt about me earlier, before my awful breakup, then I would've jumped in.

I would've broken up with my ex immediately to be with him.

"So, is that what I should do now? Now that things are sort of reversed?" I ask.

"What do you mean?"

"I mean, now that he's the one in the relationship. Should I just put it all out there? Tell him how I feel. Leave it all on the table, so to speak."

Caroline takes a moment to think about this.

I appreciate it because I know how little she thinks of him.

"Because I don't know if I can," I add quietly.

"Maybe that's your answer right there," Caroline finally says. "If you did want him, really want him to be yours, then you wouldn't be able to not to. You'd have to tell him."

I go back into my dressing room and pull the curtain closed.

I look at myself in the mirror.

The pale girl with green eyes and long dark hair is a coward.

She is afraid of life.

Afraid to really live.

Would this ever change?

CHAPTER 4 - ELLIE

WHEN YOU DECIDE TO LIVE
YOUR LIFE...

"*A*re you ready?" Caroline bursts into my room. "Our cab is downstairs."

No, I'm not ready.

Not at all.

But I'm going.

I take one last look in the mirror and grab my suitcase.

As the cab driver loads our bags into the trunk, Caroline takes my hand, giddy with excitement.

Excited is not how I would describe my state of being.

More like reluctant.

And terrified.

When I get into the cab, my stomach drops and I feel like I'm going to throw up.

But then the feeling passes.

"I can't believe this is actually happening," I say.

"I know, right? I'm so happy you're doing this with me, Ellie. I mean, really. I don't know if I could go by myself."

After ten minutes of meandering through the convoluted streets of lower Manhattan, the cab drops us off in front of a nondescript office building.

"Is the party here?" I ask.

Caroline shakes her head with a little smile on her face.

She knows something I don't know.

I can tell by that mischievous look on her face.

"What's going on?" I ask.

But she doesn't give in.

Instead, she just nudges me inside toward the security guard at the front desk.

She hands him a card, he nods, and shows us to the elevator.

"Top floor," he says.

When we reach the top floor, the elevator doors swing open on the roof and a strong gust of wind knocks into me.

Out of the corner of my eye, I see it.

The helicopter.

The blades are already going.

A man approaches us and takes our bags.

"What are we doing here?" I yell on top of my lungs.

But Caroline doesn't hear me.

I follow her inside the helicopter, ducking my head to make sure that I get in all in one piece.

A few minutes later, we take off.

We fly high above Manhattan, maneuvering past the buildings as if we're birds.

I've never been in a helicopter before and, a part of me, wishes that I'd had some time to process this beforehand.

"I didn't tell you because I thought you would freak," Caroline says into her headset.

She knows me too well.

She pulls out her phone and we pose for a few selfies.

"It's beautiful up here," I say looking out the window.

In the afternoon sun, the Manhattan skyline is breathtaking.

The yellowish red glow bounces off the glass buildings and shimmers in the twilight.

I don't know where we are going, but for the first time in a long time, I don't care.

I stay in the moment and enjoy it for everything it's worth.

Quickly the skyscrapers and the endless parade of bridges disappear and all that remains below us is the glistening of the deep blue sea.

And then suddenly, somewhere in the distance I see it.

The yacht.

At first, it appears as barely a speck on the horizon.

But as we fly closer, it grows in size.

By the time we land, it seems to be the size of its own island.

* * *

A TALL, beautiful woman waves to us as we get off the helicopter.

She's holding a plate with glasses of champagne and nods to a man in a tuxedo next to her to take our bags.

"Wow, that was quite an entrance," Caroline says to me.

"Mr. Black knows how to welcome his guests," the woman says. "My name is Lizbeth and I am here to serve you."

Lizbeth shows us around the yacht and to our stateroom.

"There will be cocktails right outside when you're ready," Lizbeth said before leaving us alone.

As soon as she left, we grabbed hands and let out a big yelp.

"Oh my God! Can you believe this place?" Caroline asks.

"No, it's amazing," I say, running over to the balcony. The blueness of the ocean stretched out as far as the eye could see.

"Are you going to change for cocktails?" Caroline asks, sitting down at the vanity. "The helicopter did a number on my hair."

We both crack up laughing.

Neither of us have ever been on a helicopter before – let alone a boat this big.

I decide against a change of clothes – my Nordstrom leggings and polka dot blouse should do just fine for cocktail hour.

But I do slip off my pair of flats and put on a nice pair of pumps, to dress up the outfit a little bit.

While Caroline changes into her short black dress, I brush the tangles out of my hair and reapply my lipstick.

"Ready?" Caroline asks.

Can't wait to read more? **One-Click BLACK EDGE Now!**

CONNECT WITH CHARLOTTE BYRD

*S*ign up for my **newsletter** to find out when I have new books!

You can also join my Facebook group, **Charlotte Byrd's Steamy Reads**, for exclusive giveaways and sneak peaks of future books.

I appreciate you sharing my books and telling your friends about them. Reviews help readers find my books! Please leave a review on your favorite site.

BLACK EDGE SERIES READING ORDER

We don't belong together.

I should have never seen him again after our first night together. But I crave him.

I'm addicted to him. He is my dark pleasure.

Mr. Black is Aiden. Aiden is Mr. Black. Two sides of the same person.

Aiden is kind and sweet. **Mr. Black is demanding and rule-oriented.**

When he invites me back to his yacht, I can't say no.

Another auction. Another bid.

I'm supposed to be his. But then everything goes wrong....

1-Click Black Rules Now!

* * *

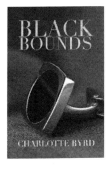

I don't belong with her.

Born into darkness, life made me a cynic incapable of love.

But then Ellie waltzed in. Innocent, optimistic, kind.

She's the opposite of what I deserve.

I bought her, but she she stole my heart.

Now my business is going up in flames.

I have only one chance to make it right.

That's where it happens...something I can never take back.

I don't cheat on her. There's no one else.

It's worse than that. Much worse.

Can we survive this?

1-Click BLACK BOUNDS Now!

* * *

They can take everything from me, but they can't take her.

Mr. Black is coming back. With a vengeance.

"I need you to sign a contract."

"What kind of contract?"

"A contract that will make you mine."

This time she's going to do everything...

1-Click BLACK CONTRACT Now!

* * *

Is this the end of us?

I found a woman I can't live without.

We've been through so much. We've had our set backs. But our love is stronger than ever.

We are survivors.

But when they take her from me at the altar, right before she is to become my wife, everything breaks.

I will do anything to free her. I will do anything to make her mine for good.

But is that enough? And what if it's not?

1-Click BLACK LIMIT Now!

* * *

Debt Series (can be read in any order)

I owe him a debt. A big one.

A **dark and dangerous** stranger paid for my mother's cancer treatment, saving her life.

Now I owe him. But I can't pay it back with money, not that I even have any.

He wants only one thing: Me.

His for one year.

Will I walk away in one piece?

1-Click DEBT Now!

DEBT

OFFER

UNKNOWN

WEALTH

ABOUT CHARLOTTE BYRD

Charlotte Byrd is the bestselling author of many contemporary romance novels. She lives in Southern California with her husband, son, and a crazy toy Australian Shepherd. She loves books, hot weather and crystal blue waters.

Write her here:

charlotte@charlotte-byrd.com

Check out her books here:

www.charlotte-byrd.com

Connect with her here:

www.facebook.com/charlottebyrdbooks

Instagram: @charlottebyrdbooks

Twitter: @ByrdAuthor

Facebook Group: Charlotte Byrd's Steamy Reads

Newsletter

Made in the USA
Las Vegas, NV
08 December 2023

82326720R00187